THE ART OF STAR WARS: EPISODE III REVENGE OF THE SITH

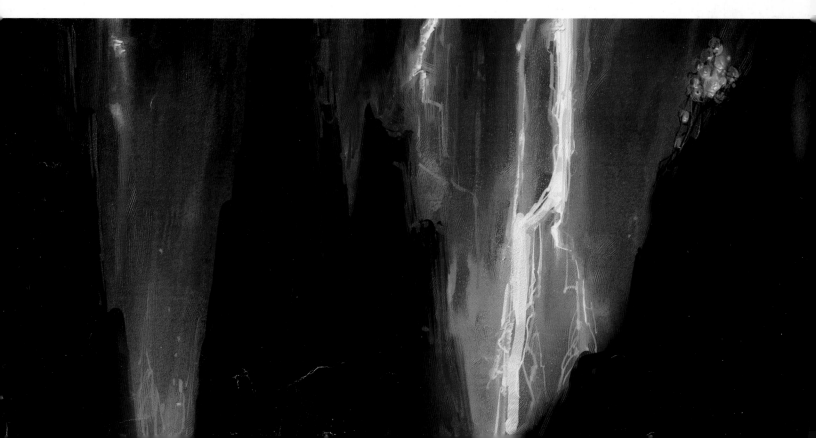

Published in the United States by Del Rey Books, an imprint of The Random House Publishing Group, a division of Random House, Inc., New York.

Del Rey is a registered trademark and the Del Rey colophon is a trademark of Random House, Inc.

◀ MUSTAFAR, VOLCANIC CLIFFS & PEAKS
Tiemens

▼ YODA ARRIVES ON DAGOBAH
Tiemens

LIBRARY OF CONGRESS CATALOGING-IN-PUBLICATION DATA IS AVAILABLE UPON REQUEST.

ISBN 0-345-43135-9

Printed in the United States of America

Del Rey Books website address: www.delreybooks.com

2 4 6 8 9 7 5 3 1

First Edition

Ballantine Books
New York, NY

To Geneviéve, Judith, and Sarah

THE ART OF
STAR WARS: EPISODE III
REVENGE OF THE SITH

Written by J. W. Rinzler

FOREWORD

DESIGN HAS ALWAYS BEEN A CRITICAL ELEMENT OF THE *STAR WARS* FILMS. On a micro level, every aspect of the galaxy –from costumes, weapons, and vehicles to alien species and remote planets –must be created from scratch. On a macro level, even the very look and feel of the film involves an intricate design process. Color palette, composition, and lighting all have a profound impact on the emotional resonance of every scene. With so much of the film now created digitally, the importance of design and pre-visualization has never been greater.

As the bridge between the original *Star Wars* Trilogy and the prequels, Episode III presented some unique design challenges. The film forced us to visualize many aspects of *Star Wars* that have been known to the audience for over 27 years but never before seen. We knew that Darth Vader was "more machine than man," but we had never seen what that meant—or how it came to be. We knew that Chewbacca came from a Wookiee world and Princess Leia from Alderaan (the one planet actually destroyed by the Death Star in *A New Hope*), but had never really seen either planet up close. And we knew that Anakin Skywalker and Obi-Wan Kenobi had a fateful confrontation on a volcano planet that—even with its near-legendary status in *Star Wars* lore—had never been glimpsed before.

All of these ideas began in my head, but they would never have found expression without the talents and insights of the many artists who have worked on the films. The group has evolved over the years. For *Revenge of the Sith*, it included artists and designers like Gavin Bocquet, Trisha Biggar, and Ian McCaig, whose work spans all of the prequels. Ryan Church and Erik Tiemens, who joined the art department on Episode II, continued their extraordinary contributions on Episode III. Rounding out the group this time was a number of gifted young artists new to *Star Wars*. Collaborating with all of them has been one of my greatest joys in making Episode III. This book is a tribute to their amazing work–often taken for granted once the film is complete–but without which there would be no film at all.

GEORGE LUCAS, DECEMBER 13, 2004
Skywalker Ranch, Marin County, California

▲ Baron N. Papanoida
Jun

▼ Alderaan
Tiemens

INTRODUCTION

GEORGE LUCAS MAKES MOVIES THE WAY HE MADE DOCUMENTARIES. When he was a graduate student at the University of Southern California, he shot a short-subject documentary about a radio disc jockey known as *The Emperor* (1967); two years later, he made a making-of documentary about Francis Ford Coppola's *The Rain People*. For each, Lucas would conceptualize, shoot, edit, write, shoot, edit, and so on, until the films took on their final forms and stories. He was able to continue this process to some degree while making his first three feature films, *THX 1138* (1971), *American Graffiti* (1973), and *Star Wars* (1977). The latter's climax, for example, came to include a threat to the Rebel base only late in the editorial process.

Many films have last-minute additions and changes, but usually these are born out of necessity. The difference between Lucas and most filmmakers is that his methodology *requires* that much of the movie be crafted in editorial. For him, the script itself is a draft of the movie, principal photography is another draft, and the rough cuts are subsequent drafts. As each element is completed, the story is honed, new scenes are introduced, and others discarded. Early in his career Lucas had to fight the studios in order to create movies this way, but with the success and independence he'd acquired by 1995, he began the *Star Wars* prequel trilogy with an unprecedented amount of control. By spring 2002, with the transition to digital moviemaking completed—and its consequential creative freedom—Lucas began work on Episode III with an even greater potential for spontaneity. As his longtime sound designer and coeditor Ben Burtt points out, in the history of cinema, only Charlie Chaplin had a similar kind of mastery over a big-budget movie.

This exacting involvement begins in the art department. It is here that Lucas repairs every Friday during preproduction. From April 2002 to June 2003, it is where he will work with a growing number of incredibly talented conceptual artists as he simultaneously writes the script. Although he'll stick to pencil and paper, the artists will work almost exclusively in the digital format. Because the software programs are now so flexible, with the exception of storyboards and sculptures, nearly every preproduction artwork reproduced in Part I of this book

(continued)

▲ CATAMARAN, POINT-OF-VIEW
Church

exists as a digital file. But this is only inverse proof of what Lucas often points out—that photography has become painting—as painting has become digital. In fact, the digital medium is the hybrid descendent of both painting and photography.

Part II is taken up primarily with the artistry of the sets, costumes, and creatures. Part III centers once again on the creation of digital artworks, this time during the postproduction phase. Because of the way Lucas works, not only does innovation and conceptual development continue during this period with earlier ideas, but new designs are continually introduced. The third part of the book thus sees the melding of principal photography, concept art, digital matte painting, and computer animation.

Taken as a whole, Parts I to III are somewhat unusual in that they're in chronological order; *The Art of Revenge of the Sith* follows Lucas's moviemaking style step-by-step in order to give readers a genuine look at how the film comes together. In this way, the nearly three-year visual history of planets, characters, costumes, scenes, vehicles—all the elements of the entire film—is plainly revealed. While a few concepts will be seen bursting into existence in one artwork, and ending up in the film more or less unaltered, the majority of concepts will be seen morphing into other concepts, combining with still others, separating, and migrating until they fit into Lucas's final vision. *The Art of Star Wars: Episode III Revenge of the Sith* is also a companion book to *The Making of Star Wars: Revenge of the Sith*. Because both books are organized chronologically, they can be used complementarily.

The two books combine to present the efforts of a thousand artists, artisans, and technicians all working in conjunction with George Lucas. Hopefully those who see the film will review these pages afterward to get a longer look at the fantastic imaginings they just saw in passing. . . .

▼ MUSTAFAR MONSTER
Jun

Trisha Biggar
costume designer,
Australia (Aus)

Gavin Bocquet
production designer, Aus

Robert Barnes
concept artist-sculptor,
Skywalker Ranch (SR)

Ryan Church
concept design supervisor, SR

Rob Coleman
animation director,
Industrial Light & Magic (ILM)

Matt Connors
head scenic artist, Aus

Ivo Coveney
costume props supervisor, Aus

David Craig
concept researcher, SR

Stian Dahlslett
costume concept artist, Aus

Fay David
art department supervisor, SR

Yanick Dusseault
digital matte artist, ILM

Dave Elsey
creatures shop creative
supervisor, Aus

T. J. Frame
concept artist, SR

Warren Fu
concept artist, SR

John Goodson
concept model-maker, SR

Ian Gracie
art director, Aus

Greg Hajdu
construction manager, Aus

Jonathan Harb
digital matte painting supervisor,
ILM

Phil Harvey
art director, Aus

Alex Jaeger
concept artist/art director,
SR/ILM

Sang Jun Lee
concept artist, SR

Jacinta Leong
assistant art director, Aus

Stephanie Lostimolo
art department assistant, SR

George Lucas
writer-director, SR

Toshiyuki Maeda
digital matte artist, ILM

Stephan Martiniére
concept artist, SR

Aaron McBride
art director, ILM

Iain McCaig
concept artist, SR

Rick McCallum
producer, SR

Glen McIntosh
lead animator, ILM

Richard Miller
sculptor, ILM

Michael Patrick Murnane
concept artist-sculptor, SR

Brett Northcutt
digital matte artist, ILM

Peter Russell
supervising art director, Aus

Gert Stevens
concept artist, Aus

Erik Tiemens
concept design supervisor, SR

Derek Thompson
concept artist, SR

Johan Thorngren
digital matte artist, ILM

Danny Wagner
concept sculptor/model-maker, SR/ILM

Feng Zhu
concept artist, SR

Note: *For a complete list of cast and crew, and many short biographies of same, go to* **starwars.com.**

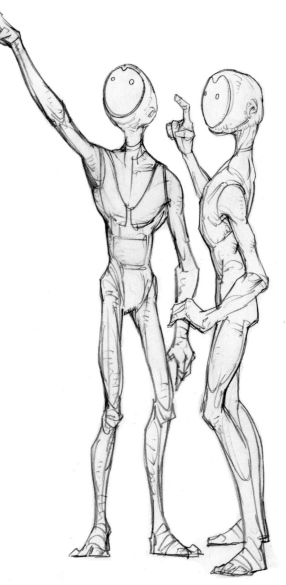

▶ POLIS MASSANS
Jun

contents

▲ SINKHOLE WITH TANK (Tiemens); SPEEDER CONCEPT (Church)
MUSTAFAR INTERIOR (Zhu); HOSTAGE SHIP, CORRIDOR BATTLE 02 (Church)

◀▶ NABOO ORNAMENTAL DESIGNS THROUGHOUT BOOK BY Stephanie Lostimolo

PART I–PREPRODUCTION

About a month before *Star Wars*: Episode II *Attack of the Clones* is released on May 16, 2002, writer-director George Lucas starts work on Episode III. As he has done for each of the prequel trilogy films, he begins by providing a

few story ideas to his concept art department, located on the grounds of Skywalker Ranch in northern California. As of the summer of 2002, though its ranks will grow, this department consists of concept design supervisors Erik Tiemens and Ryan Church, and art department supervisor Fay David. On June 7, they present Lucas and producer Rick McCallum with the first of what will become a three-year avalanche of brilliant and imaginative concept art for the last and most climactic *Star Wars* film. . . .

▲ ALDERAAN, ALPINE FALL COLORS (Tiemens); CRYSTAL WORLD (Church)
NEIMOIDIAN INTERIOR 02 (Church)

▶ SINKHOLE ARCHITECTURE 05
Church

▲ RING PLANET
Church

▼ ROUGH GESSO BLUE CLIFFS
Tiemens

▶ CRYSTAL PLANET, IDEA 02 (INSET)
Martiniére

JUNE 7, 2002

George Lucas's initial assignment is to create seven planets for seven Clone War battlefields to serve as the opening of the film. Art department meetings are held each Friday, and at the first gathering, some of the designs revealed represent new ideas–such as a ring world and a crystal world–while other planets have their origins in concept art created decades ago for the first trilogy: for example, a sinkhole planet (earlier called Crevasse City) and a volcano planet (originally conceived of as Darth Vader's home).

"Now is the time to go way out there—to be as wild as possible."—GEORGE LUCAS

▲ CRYSTAL PLANET, IDEA 01
Martiniére

"George casually says to us, 'Oh, you guys, I want you to start thinking about seven planets—seven new planets that are completely different from each other—this is where the Clone Wars are happening.'"—RYAN CHURCH

▲ BRIDGE PLANET
Church

▶ CRYSTAL WORLD
Church

◀▲ CRYSTALIZED ICEBERG PLANET
Tiemens

"I had some ideas for a crystalized iceberg planet, which was a great starting point, because George said he'd like to do something more with crystals."—ERIK TIEMENS

▲ SINKHOLE PLANET SHOT DESIGNS
Tiemens

▼ REEF PLANET
Tiemens

▲ SINKHOLE PLANET
Tiemens

▲ INTO THE FIRE
Tiemens

▼ VOLCANO PLANET (MUFASTA)
Church

"I thought it would it be cool—though it's clearly not in the movie—to see Star Destroyers heading toward their destruction on Mufasta." —TIEMENS

MUFASTA, THE VOLCANO PLANET

JUNE 7, 2002

After Lucas chooses reference photos and concept art created for earlier *Star Wars* films of the volcano planet, Church and Tiemens begin to explore what will be a key—if not the most important—environment for Episode III.

▼ MUFASTA TOWERS
Tiemens

▲ MUFASTA CONCEPT PAINTINGS 02 & 03
Tiemens

▲ SHIPS ABOVE SINKHOLE PLANET (WITH MCQUARRIE BEEHIVE MOUNTAINS & JOE JOHNSTON SHIP)
Tiemens

▲ AERIAL BATTLE (OVER CORUSCANT)
Church

▲ AERIAL BATTLE 02 (OVER CORUSCANT)
Church

▲ CRYSTAL WORLD BATTLE
Church

CLONE WARS I

JUNE 7–21, 2002

At this point in the making of Episode III, there is no script. The contexts for these lethal struggles between the Separatists—led by Count Dooku and his armies of battle droids—and the Galactic Republic—led by Supreme Chancellor Palpatine, his Jedi generals, and their clone armies—come from the minds of the painters, as inspired by story fragments provided by Lucas. During one of the first meetings, he mentions that Kashyyyk, the Wookiee homeworld, will most likely appear in the film, so that planet becomes a possible locale for a Clone War.

"From the very beginning, we were painting scenes that had a context. I thought, What if a bunch of bad guys were attacking Padmé and the clones, who are trying to get back to their ship [above]. I also thought it'd be cool to have Wookiees versus clone troopers—actually it was with clone troopers at this point [below]."—CHURCH

▼ KASHYYYK BATTLE PAINTING
Church

▲ SINKHOLE BATTLE, VERSION 03
Tiemens

machines at war

JUNE 7–21, 2002

Because Lucas has noted that in these seven Clone War battles the Separatists are still using droid armies, Church sets to work creating new droids and new vessels. The Republic will also have new weapons, and first among these is an updated Jedi starfighter, the early version of which was seen in *Attack of the Clones*. At the June 11, 2002, meeting, visiting production designer Gavin Bocquet and Lucas discuss how much of the starfighter will have to be built and how much can be created digitally.

"At first George didn't go for it, but it came back later as the buzz droid. He was worried about functionality, but now its form makes perfect sense."—CHURCH

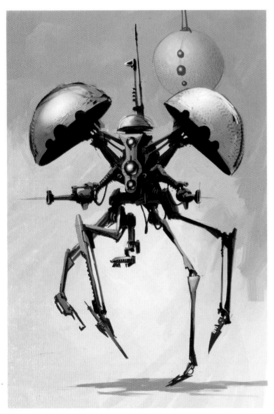

▲ FLOATING DROID CONCEPT 01 (PROTO BUZZ DROID)
Church

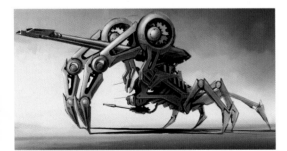

▲ ATTACK DROID CONCEPT
Church

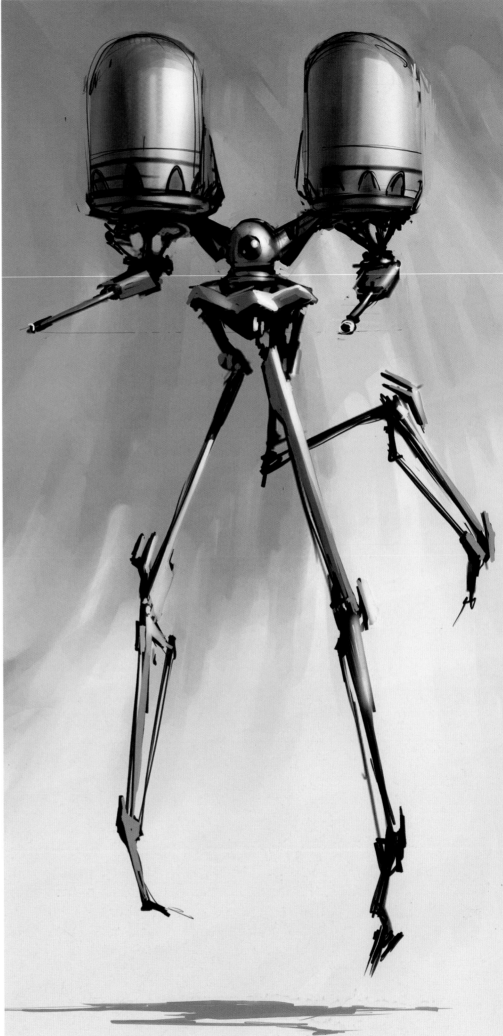

▲ FLOATING DROID CONCEPT 02
Church

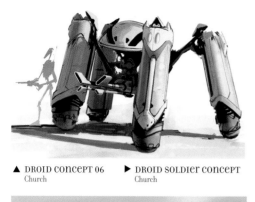

▲ DROID CONCEPT 06
Church

▶ DROID SOLDIER CONCEPT
Church

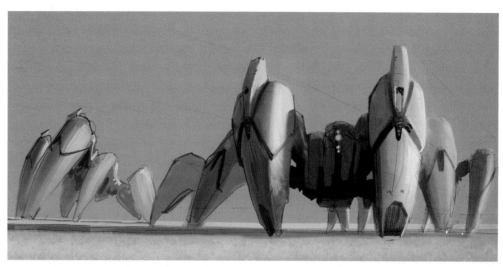

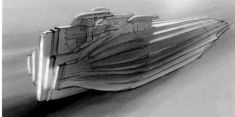

▲ SHIP CONCEPT 03
Church

▲ VEHICLE CONCEPT 05
Church

"George told me he wanted the starfighter's wings to pop open [below]. He wanted to see a lot more guns on it, too. I dropped them down the middle, which created a great sight line."—CHURCH

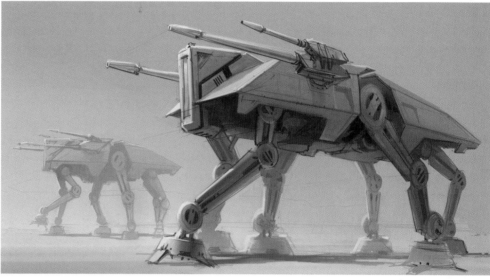

▲ WALKER CONCEPT
Church

▲ JEDI STARFIGHTER VERSION 03, AFT R2 UNIT
Church

▲ JEDI STARFIGHTER, VERSION 05
Church

21

▲ FEMALE LEMUR CONCEPT
Tiemens

▲ LEMUR CONCEPT, VERSION 04
Tiemens

JUNE 21–JULY 10, 2002

At the June 21, 2002, meeting, Lucas asks for a lizard to be created, based on an old *Star Wars* trading card by Al Williamson. This assignment goes to concept artist and sculptor Robert Barnes. Tiemens is asked to work on the lemur people. When the first ones are presented at the July 10 gathering, Lucas asks for more color variations and costume designs. During all these meetings, Lucas carries with him an "OK" stamp. If stamped "OK," a concept is approved for further exploration. A much more rarely used stamp is "FABULOUSO," reserved for those concepts that Lucas deems perfect as is.

▲▶ ANAKIN ON LIZARD CREATURE
Barnes

"He liked the neck of one lizard [right] *and the body of another* [above]. *Then George brought up the idea of the lizard having feathers. For the trooper one* [below], *I was really inspired by pictures of GIs accompanied by German shepherds wearing food packs."*—ROBERT E. BARNES

◀ LEMUR CREATURE, VERSIONS 02 & 03 (INSET)
Tiemens

▲ CLONE TROOPERS AND SUPPLY BEASTS
Barnes

JULY 19–26, 2002

Throughout preproduction—and beyond—the artists and Lucas revisit and refine the details of approved planets, creatures, and so on. Ultimately, some concepts are combined, while others are abandoned. Freelance concept artist Stephan Martiniére, who began in June, continues to help in the creation of new environments. "I would tell them about a scene, an animal, or a character," Lucas explains, "and they would do a bunch of designs. I would okay some or modify or change them, and we build; we go to the next thing. And so, every week, they get more to design. Some of these guys are designing costumes; some of them are designing sets; some of them are designing props or cars. And then I'm writing the script."

"We're revisiting bridgeworld [above & right]. Because George liked the idea of bridges, I wanted to put it on a less generic planet."—CHURCH

▲ BRIDGE WORLD, REVISED
Church

▼ BRIDGE PLANET CHASE
Church

▼ CRYSTAL WORLD ARCHITECTURE VERSION 05
Church

▼ CRYSTAL PLANET MEDIUM SHOT 03
Martiniére

clone wars II

JULY 19–26, 2002

For each art department meeting, the artists print out their digital paintings and pin them to foam core boards. Lucas then examines them board by board. The whole process can take anywhere from twenty minutes to more than an hour, depending on the quantity and the complexity of the ideas being presented. Church's "Sinkhole Street Level" receives the first FABULOUSO of Episode III.

▲ CATHEDRAL BATTLE, REVISED
Church

▼ SINKHOLE, STREET LEVEL
Church

"George liked the shot design. It's droids versus Jedi; bad guys on the left, good guys on the right. Compositionally, your eyes are drawn straight to that green lightsaber."—CHURCH

"This was the first of many instances when George said, 'It looks like a set [below]. Open it up [left].'"
—CHURCH

▼ CATHEDRAL BATTLE
Church

▲ MUFASTA BATTLE CONCEPT
Tiemens

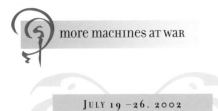

Because the film is still in embryonic form, many early vehicle designs will be assigned drivers much later in the process. "Vehicle concept 10," for example, will eventually be given to a certain Separatist general. After an overall vehicle look is approved, concept model-maker John Goodson takes them to the next stage: three-dimensionality.

▲ ROTOR SHIP (PADDLE WHEEL)
Tiemens

▲ VEHICLE CONCEPT 10
Church

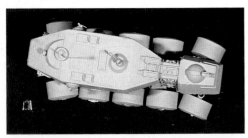

"My idea for the paddle-wheel ship was to give it an older, nautical feel."—TIEMENS

▲ GUNSHIP
Tiemens

▲ CLONE TANK MODEL (JOE JOHNSTON CONCEPT)
Goodson

▼ STARFIGHTER MODEL
Goodson

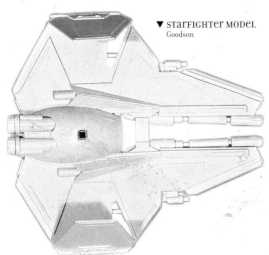

▲ DROID CONCEPT VERSION 01
Tiemens

▼ ALDERAAN STUDY
Tiemens

▲ COLOR SCRIPT VERSION 10 (MYGEETO)
Tiemens

▼ ALDERAAN CONCEPT
Church

seven-planet craft

While none of these vehicles will make it into the movie as is, many of them have parts that will be recycled into future final designs. "Vehicle concept 01" and the "fighter concept" will become the ARC-170 clone fighter; the "ribbon ship" will find its way into the Wookiee arsenal. As of August 2, 2002, two more concept artists join the team on a freelance basis: Feng Zhu and T. J. Frame.

▲ VEHICLE CONCEPT 01
Church

▲ FIGHTER CONCEPT
Church

"The X-wing is all-nose, so I moved the whole fuselage back to the middle point. I rounded off the corners and hung huge, clumsy guns on it [left]. George knocked the tail off recently."
—CHURCH

▲ DUAL LASER AIRSPEEDER
Tiemens

▲ DEATH DROID
Zhu

▲ SUPPLY DROID
Zhu

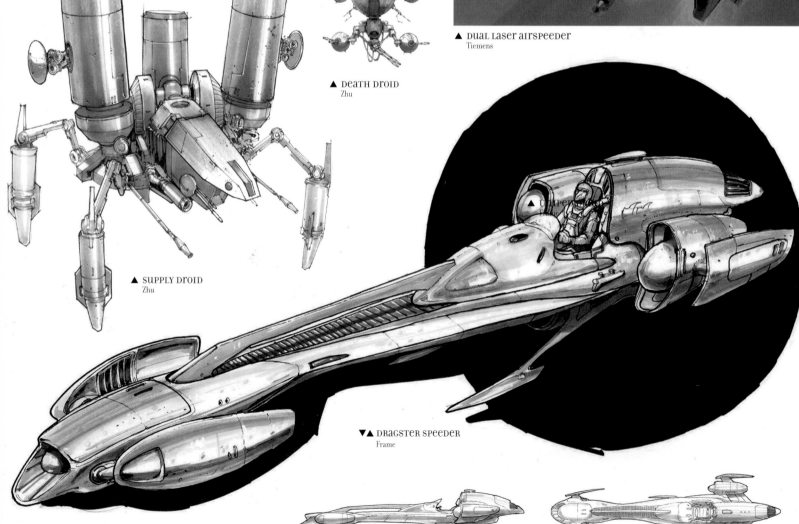

▲ UMPERWERAL
Frame

▼▲ DRAGSTER SPEEDER
Frame

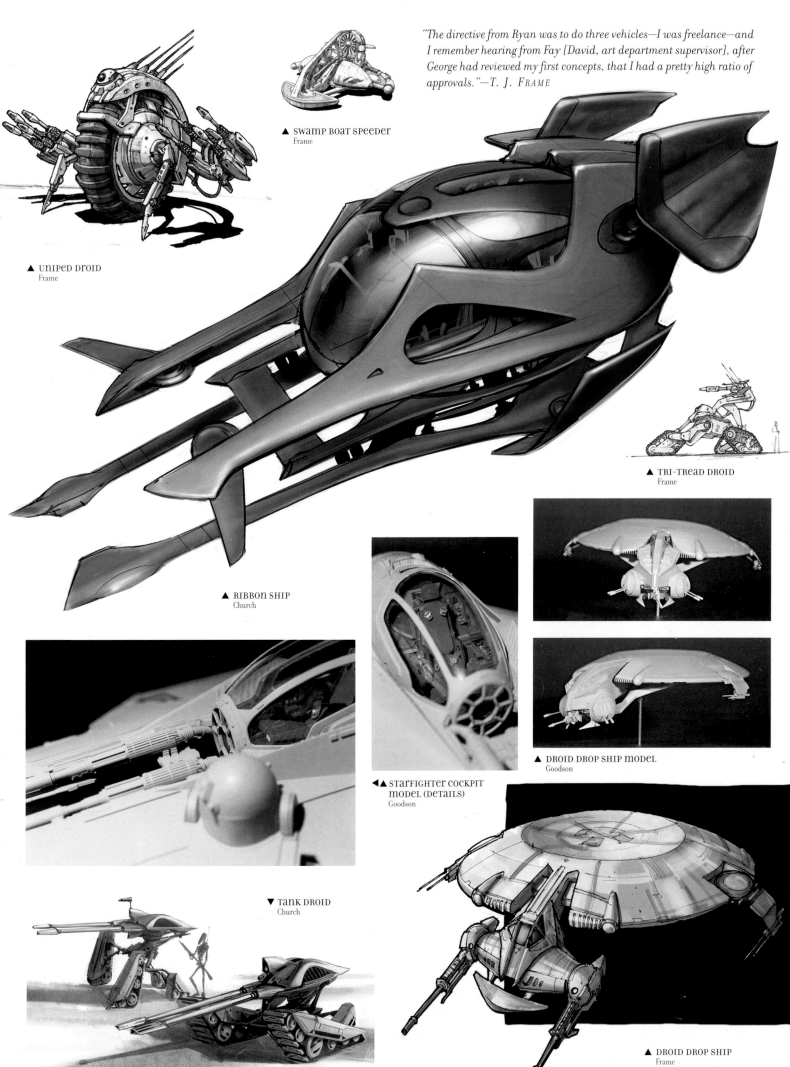

▲ SWAMP BOAT SPEEDER
Frame

"The directive from Ryan was to do three vehicles—I was freelance—and I remember hearing from Fay [David, art department supervisor], after George had reviewed my first concepts, that I had a pretty high ratio of approvals."—T. J. FRAME

▲ UNIPED DROID
Frame

▲ TRI-TREAD DROID
Frame

▲ RIBBON SHIP
Church

◀▲ STARFIGHTER COCKPIT MODEL (DETAILS)
Goodson

▲ DROID DROP SHIP MODEL
Goodson

▼ TANK DROID
Church

▲ DROID DROP SHIP
Frame

◀ PADMÉ COSTUME 09
Jun

▲ LEMUR SCULPTURES
Barnes

"The design challenge with the lemurs was to take something inherently cute and give it an edge."
—BARNES

▲ LEMUR CONCEPT 05
Jun

BEAUTY AND THE BEASTS

AUGUST 2–30, 2002

A new member of the art department, Sang Jun Lee (Jun), has been brought in to work on creatures and costume designs. The artist shows designs for Padmé, and Lucas indicates that she'll need something to wear that's more Senatorial. She'll also need action and casual wear. A key announcement is also made: Principal photography will begin on June 25, 2003, which starts a ticking clock for the art department. By that date, and well before, the majority of its work needs to be done—in particular, the costumes, since costume designer Trisha Biggar and her team are slated for a November 2002 start.

▶ LEMUR CONCEPT 13
Jun

◀ PADMÉ COSTUME 03
Jun

▲ LEMUR CONCEPT 06
Jun

▲ LEMUR CONCEPT 04
Jun

◀ LEMUR CONCEPT 11
Jun

"In San Francisco, on Nineteenth Street, there was a zoo exhibition flag that had two lemurs on it, which George saw. He called Fay [David] right away and said, 'I saw a poster with a lemur. It'd be a good idea to build a character up from there.'"—SANG JUN LEE

▶ LEMUR CONCEPT 15
Jun

AUGUST 2–30, 2002

Armed with the knowledge that the fabled Wookiee homeworld might appear in the film and that the Clone Wars are raging, Church and Tiemens embark on a series of battle paintings for Kashyyyk. Lucas approves the Wookiee flying catamaran, the lagoon concept, and a giant tree room; the flying saucers, however, are moved back to Alderaan.

◀ WOOKIEE FIGHTER (ORNITHOPTER)
Church

"This was the big pitch to roll together everything we knew about Kashyyyk into one painting [below]. I put those ornithopter choppers in there; this beautiful exaggerated landscape; those cantilevered trees; and the tank vehicles I'd designed from Episode II." — CHURCH

"When you're under deadline, it's very easy to lose your temper, but that didn't happen once—instead, there was a lot of laughter coming from the back room."—FAY DAVID

▲ KASHYYYK BATTLE 02
Church

▲ GIANT TREE ROOM
Tiemens

▼ WOOKIEE VILLAGE SKETCH
Tiemens

▶ KASHYYYK BATTLE
Church

▲ WOOKIEE VILLAGE, VERSION 01
Tiemens

"I painted Padmé walking with some Wookiees, though I had no idea what the story was. I was playing with scale." —TIEMENS

◄ KASHYYYK LANDING
Church

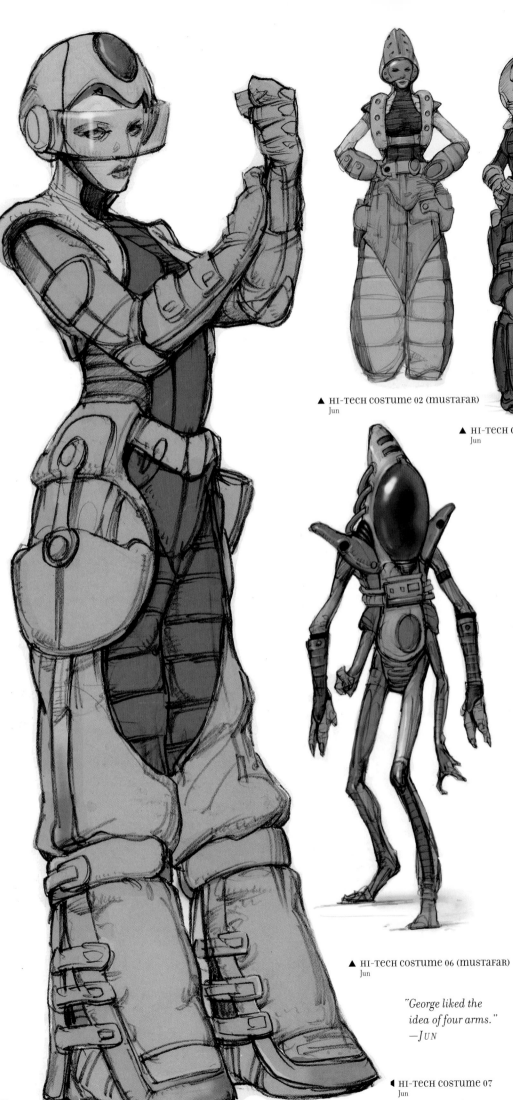

▲ HI-TECH COSTUME 02 (mustafar)
Jun

▲ HI-TECH COSTUME 05 (mustafar)
Jun

▲ HI-TECH COSTUME 01 (mustafar)
Jun

"Because they live on Mustafar with the lava and the gas, I designed the costumes to be really thick to protect their bodies."—Jun

creature & costume concepts

SEPTEMBER 5–27, 2002

With planets such as Mustafar (as Mufasta is renamed) and Mygeeto now fixed as players in the film, Jun receives the task of populating them with aliens and creatures. The four-legged insect *[opposite page]* will eventually metamorphose into the "Jun bug" and feature in an establishing shot of the volcano planet.

▲ HI-TECH COSTUME 06 (mustafar)
Jun

"George liked the idea of four arms."
—Jun

◀ HI-TECH COSTUME 07
Jun

▲ CREATURE CONCEPTS
Jun

◄ CRYSTAL ALIEN 01, FULL BODY
Jun

▶ CREATURE CONCEPT 02
Jun

▲ CRYSTAL ALIEN 01, HEAD DETAIL
Jun

▲ CREATURE CONCEPT (MUSTAFAR)
Jun

"I don't know what it is, but it looks good."—LUCAS

▼ CREATURE CONCEPT (JUN BUG)
Jun

▲ CRYSTAL MONSTER (MYGEETO)
Jun

"George said, 'That's too much, but good try.'"—JUN

SEPTEMBER 5–27, 2002

Lucas's further commentary on Alderaan is that its architecture is ultramodern. As directed, Church and Tiemens have added flying saucers into the environment. As for the ring world, Lucas would like the rings to be less uniform, as if they've evolved over hundreds of years, but he okays the fishbone structure. Artists are also creating interiors for the approved planets. Both Zhu and Frame have joined the in-house art department to help in these endeavors.

▲ RING WORLD, POINT-OF-VIEW
Church

▼ KASHYYYK SKYDOCK
Church

▲ RING WORLD, REVISED
Church

▲ KASHYYYK CITY
Church

"George had mentioned the Swiss Family Robinson, so I was really happy with this one [right]; I really got into it."—CHURCH

▲ ALDERAAN SAUCER PLATFORM
Church

▲ CITY, FRESNEL INTERIOR–CRYSTAL WORLD
Church

"[Alderaan is] an incredible technological event in the middle of the countryside. Very concentrated, ultramodern."—LUCAS

▼ ALDERAAN STUDIES
Tiemens

▶ ALDERAAN SUPER TOWER STUDY
Tiemens

"This was a lot of fun because you had the challenge of drawing buildings upside down."—FENG ZHU

▼ BRIDGE WORLD, VERSION 03
Zhu

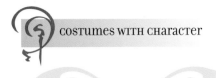

OCTOBER 4–31, 2002

Veteran concept artist Iain McCaig joins the art department on October 4, 2002. Jun receives three FABULOUSOS on the same day for his Alderaan costume concepts, which meet perfectly with Lucas's vision of a high-tech society. Their high marks also mean costume designer Trisha Biggar can start work on them.

"It was great getting the FABULOUSOS. Rick [McCallum] was there and he shook my hand."—JUN

▼ COSTUME CONCEPT 06
Jun

▲ COSTUME CONCEPTS 01 & 07
Jun

▲ COSTUME CONCEPTS
13 & 16
Jun

▲ COSTUME CONCEPT 08
Jun

▲ FEMALE
COSTUME
CONCEPT 01
Jun

▲ PADMÉ 01
McCaig

▶ OBI-WAN COSTUME/HEADSET CONCEPT
McCaig

▲ PADMÉ 04
McCaig

"I'd been looking at a
samurai photo where
they have this piece of
hair that comes down,
which I re-created with
Obi-Wan's headset."
—IAIN MCCAIG

FERAL GROOMING

After seeing McCaig's October 18 painting of a scarred Anakin [left], Lucas comments that Anakin will have to be more attractive for the duration of the film, because Padmé is still in love with him—and he has not yet gone over to the dark side.

▲ anakin 11
McCaig

"George wanted Anakin to look more like Qui-Gon Jinn, to show that he was going beyond what Obi-Wan was teaching him—hence the long hair."
—McCaig

▲ anakin 01
McCaig

"She's in love with a monster, so I wanted to make her courageous and strong, like a lioness. George really liked the big hair, but I'd just given Anakin the long hair, so they couldn't both have it."
—McCaig

◄ anakin emerging from volcano
McCaig

▲ padmé 11
McCaig

FIRST WORLDS AND LAST STANDS

OCTOBER 5–31, 2002

Hired to help create creatures and action scenes, newcomer Derek Thompson presents "key frames"—pivotal moments from a proposed sequence—at the October 25 meeting. At this point, the artists are still working without a script. Many of them will note afterward that, during this time, everyone was trying to get their favorite ideas into the story.

▲ BRIDGE WORLD BATTLE
Church

▲ SINKHOLE BATTLE (UTAPAU)
Church

◀ SALEUCAMI (BRIDGE WORLD) BATTLE
Church

"I based this on a Ralph McQuarrie painting. It's just a cool little scenario: they're trying to save this guy. And I wanted to show that this ship holds more than one person, like a Hellcat from World War II."—CHURCH

▲ CLONE WAR KEY FRAME 01
Thompson

▼ CLONE WAR KEY FRAME 13
Thompson

"My idea was that Anakin would actually have a team of rogue riders."—DEREK THOMPSON

▲ WALKER IN ALIEN FOREST
Church

"George said, 'We still need more planets.' So I made an organic Vietnam-style world."—CHURCH

"This is the natives' last stand—as you can see by the bloodstained trail." —CHURCH

▲ BATTLE ON MYGEETO
Church

▲ ALDERAAN INTERIOR
Church

"Since I was a kid, I've wanted to do something that was so beautiful that when you hear Alderaan is destroyed in Episode IV, you go, 'Oh, crap!'" —CHURCH

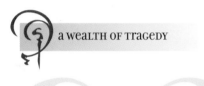

a WEALTH OF TRAGEDY

OCTOBER 5–31, 2002

In early October, ring world becomes Cato Neimoidia, homeworld of the nefarious Neimoidians, which Lucas says is a combination of opulence and high-tech. For November, Lucas requests an asteroid wasteland planet—which should look like the moon, have modern buildings, and be the home of inhabitants who wear space suits. As the planets multiply, he asks that a reference chart be created so they don't start to visually overlap. As the work increases, concept artist Alex Jaeger joins the team, first concentrating on Saleucami, formerly bridge world.

▲ ALDERAAN LANDSCAPE–FALL COLORS 04
Tiemens

▲ CRYSTAL WORLD ENVIRONMENT (MYGEETO)
Jaeger

▼ ALDERAAN CONTROL ROOM
Zhu

▼ ALDERAAN
Frame

▼ SALEUCAMI BRIDGE
Jaeger

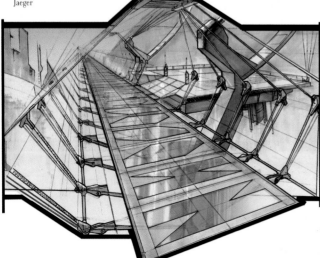

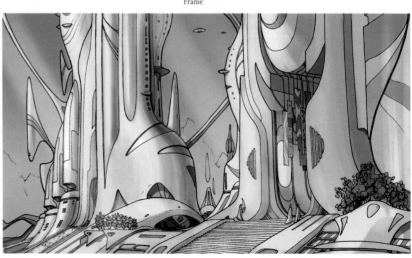

"The Neimoidian homeworld had to be gold, because they're hoarding it, and George mandated that he had to be able to see out the windows. I added a floating chandelier, and tables that walk around and ask whether you want more wine or food." —CHURCH

▲ NEIMOIDIAN FOYER
Church

▼ RING WORLD (CATO NEIMOIDIA) CONFERENCE TABLE
Frame

▼ CATO NEIMOIDIA
Zhu

▲ THORN WORLD
Church

▶ WOOKIEE CONCEPT 07
Jun

"This is Chewbacca's father. Maybe his father is a warrior, and is killed, so Chewbacca has to run away—and that's how he meets Han Solo." —JUN

WOOKIEES LIVE AGAIN

OCTOBER 25–31, 2002

As Kashyyyk is explored, Lucas okays the addition of limited technology to the Wookiee home, but cautions the artists not to make Wookiee children look like Ewoks, and to explore a Venetian look.

◀ WOOKIEE CONCEPT 04
(CHEWBACCA'S FATHER)
Jun

▲ WOOKIEE CONCEPT 03
Jun

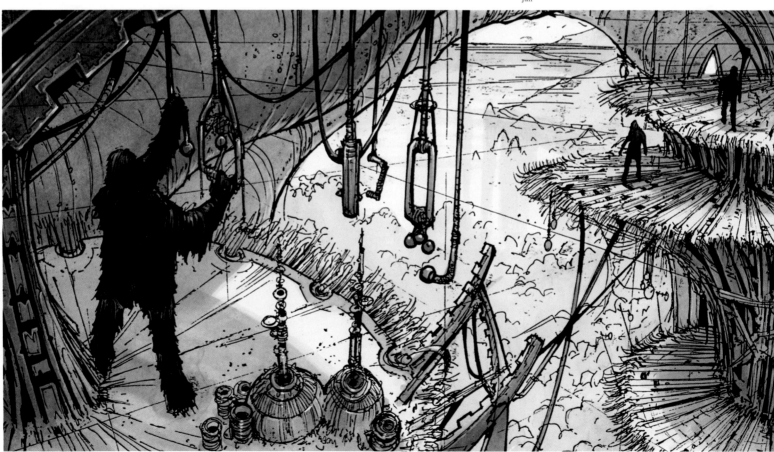

▲ KASHYYYK ENVIRONMENT
Zhu

▲ clone war key frames 02 & 14
Thompson

"We didn't want to make many predeterminations about who went where and did what, but at the same time, we wanted to generate excitement and hopefully get George excited about putting a scene together that we thought was cool."—THOMPSON

▶ wookiee warrior
Jun

▲ wookiee concept 01
Jun

▲ LIZARD CREATURE
McCaig

▲ BLASTERS
Zhu

▲ HAMMERHEAD CREATURE CONCEPT 08
Thompson

▲ LIZARD SCULPTURE
Barnes

▼ ANAKIN ON LIZARD
McCaig

▲ SINKHOLE WORLD (UTAPAU) WITH SOLDIER
Zhu

While searching for more Clone War participants, Thompson hits upon idea of introducing aliens from Episode IV's cantina scene. Lucas okays the "Hammerheads" as bad guys, but says that the film will not include the "flight-suit aliens."

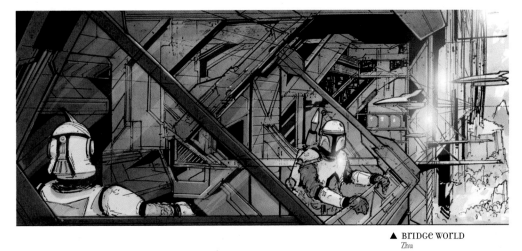

▲ BRIDGE WORLD
Zhu

"I had a grown-up Boba Fett hanging out with a clone trooper. But we thought it might be suggesting too much story to George . . ."
—ZHU

◄ TRENCH SOLDIERS
Thompson

PADMÉ'S GARDEN (VERANDA)

On October 25, Lucas divulges more of the Episode III story. A new locale is needed for a key love scene between Padmé and Anakin. Because the planet of the scene has yet to be determined, Tiemens creates a number of settings on Naboo, Padmé's homeworld. Upon seeing them, Lucas transfers the locale to Coruscant, while some of the garden elements find their way to Kashyyyk.

▲ CORUSCANT ZEN GARDEN 03
Tiemens

▼ NABOO GARDEN 06
Tiemens

"I was paying homage to George Inness, who went to Italy where he did a similar painting of a monk in a garden [below]. I was very excited to create a Romeo-and-Juliet element. It's really the stress meeting between Anakin and Padmé [right]."—TIEMENS

▲ NABOO GARDEN 11
Tiemens

▶ NABOO GARDEN 09
Tiemens

▲ MUSTAFAR BOILER ROOM DUEL
Fu

THE CLIMACTIC DUEL BEGINS

On October 25, Lucas also confirms that Anakin and Obi-Wan will fight on the planet Mustafar. The duel will take place in interiors and exteriors. He also says that the film will require a landing platform for the volcano planet. By the October 31 meeting, many ideas are already being explored, some of them by the latest member of the art department, Warren Fu.

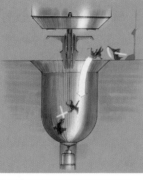

▲ MUSTAFAR FIGHT PIT ORTHO
Fu

"I thought it'd be cool to have them fall into a pit with really smooth sides and a sharp fan at the bottom. But George said it'd be too easy for them to jump out."—WARREN FU

▲ MUSTAFAR FIGHT PIT, DETAIL
Fu

▼ JEDI ON MUSTAFAR
Jaeger

▼ MUSTAFAR LANDING AREA VERSION 02
Fu

"These are old, old, old. Mufastar's been around a long time. I've always had this set-piece: the end between Obi-Wan and Anakin. I knew that's where this movie was going to end up. It's all this volcanic land, with lava shooting up, so it's monochromatic in its red-and-blackness. I've had this image with me for a long time."—LUCAS

▲ MUSTAFAR SABER DUEL
Church

▼ MUSTAFAR GENERATOR ROOM INTERIOR
Jaeger

▼ MONKEY BAR CHASE
Fu

"In a generator room [left], Anakin and Obi-Wan are jumping onto floating platforms, which aren't quite stable, as they're usually used for floating lights. So when the Jedi jump on them, the platforms start sinking.—ALEX JAEGER

▼ MUSTAFAR BUILDING 01
Zhu

▲ SEPARATIST CRUISER BREAK, REVISED HOSTAGE SHIP
Church

 SEPARATIST CRUISER GAGS

OCT 25–NOV 8, 2002

Lucas has changed the beginning of the film, as it now opens during a giant aerial battle over Coruscant. New plot points require an enormous enemy vessel in which the Separatists are holding a hostage. To get to that hostage, Anakin and Obi-Wan have to traverse many perilous pitfalls, also known as "gags."

▲ SEPARATIST CRUISER CORRIDOR BATTLE
Church

◄► "NITRO FOBOS" STUDIES FOR THE GENERATOR ROOM
Thompson

"George wanted to have these organisms living inside the fuel, which attack Anakin and Obi-Wan." —THOMPSON

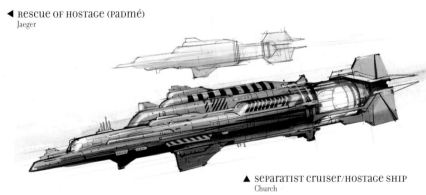

◄ RESCUE OF HOSTAGE (PADMÉ)
Jaeger

▲ SEPARATIST CRUISER/HOSTAGE SHIP
Church

◄ DROIDEKAS ON GLASS
Jaeger

"They just blocked off a door, so Anakin and Obi-Wan think they're safe—when all of a sudden they hear this little tink, tink, tink on the window [left]."
—JAEGER

▲ BREAKING GLASS
Jaeger

▲ ANAKIN RIDING LIZARD
Jun

"We didn't know where the lizard would be in the film. Iguanas can climb ninety degrees, so I thought, Let's put it in a sinkhole on a rock." —*JUN*

McCaig exhibits two key frames, one of which shows Padmé, doubled up in pain, seeking Yoda's help. "Padmé has the Force flowing through her," McCaig says. "She has more midi-chlorians than any person ever had because she's pregnant with the Skywalker twins, so I was wondering if we see her suffer." Although Lucas is enthusiastic, neither of these moments will make the final cut. Meanwhile, the production department at Elstree Studios in London, England—where production designer Gavin Bocquet and costume designer Trisha Biggar are now working—has a new member: artist Stian Dahlslett, who will work up more costume concepts.

▲ PREGNANT PADMÉ 02
McCaig

"George said there might be a scene where Padmé's doubled over in agony and Yoda is there, but unable to help her [below]."—MCCAIG

▼ KEY FRAME 02 (ANAKIN RESCUED BY DROIDS ON MUSTAFAR, IN PADMÉ'S DREAM)
McCaig

▲ ANAKIN COSTUME 01
McCaig

"We wanted to bring Anakin forward to Darth Vader—even the shape of his hair was meant to suggest Vader's black helmet [above]."—MCCAIG

◀ KEY FRAME 01, YODA & PADMÉ
McCaig

63

"On Mustafar there is no moisture, so their skin would dry out. [Concept researcher] David Craig showed me some costumes from Italy with over-lapping fabrics, so when they walk the fabrics interact, creating interesting shapes." —JUN

▲ MUSTAFAR CONCEPT 06
Jun

▲ MUSTAFAR CONCEPT 07
Jun

▲ MUSTAFAR
CONCEPT 02
Jun

◀ MUSTAFAR
CONCEPT 05
Jun

ALIEN CONCEPTS

NOVEMBER 1–8, 2002

Lucas responds once again more than favorably to Jun's creature and costume designs, fixing Mustafar concepts 02, 05, 06 & 07 as is with FABULOUSOS. He also approves a few of McCaig's Neimoidian variations.

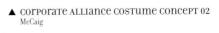

▲ CORPORATE ALLIANCE COSTUME CONCEPT 02
McCaig

▲ MUSTAFAR CONCEPTS 04 & 01
Jun

▲ ALIEN CREATURE CONCEPT 07
Jun

▲ MUSTAFAR ALIEN CONCEPT 02
Thompson

▲ NEIMOIDIAN COSTUME CONCEPTS
Dahlslett

"I thought it'd be interesting to have a four-armed Jedi." —JUN

◀▼ MUSTAFAR ALIEN/JEDI CONCEPTS 01 & 02
Jun

"This is the biggest art department I've ever worked with. And everyone is confident enough in their abilities so that we can jam the way that musicians do—and that's really rare." —McCAIG

▲ NEIMOIDIAN COSTUME CONCEPT 01
McCaig

POLIS MASSA CONTROLS
Zhu

"We didn't know what Polis Massa was for, so I thought it might be where they're building the Death Star [above]." —ZHU

▼ POLIS MAZTA 01
Tiemens

NOVEMBER 1–14, 2002

After seeing the concepts of the asteroid planet, now called Polis Massa (or early on, Mazta), on November 8, Lucas expands its size to give it a more dramatic scale and gives the artists additional ideas for the architecture. "My first painting of Polis Massa [below] is an homage to earlier science-fiction films and to *LIFE* magazine illustrations of astronauts visiting the moon [by Chesley Bonestell]," Tiemens says. "There's a protective shield to protect the base from asteroids."

◄ POLIS MASSA HALLWAY
Zhu

▼ POLIS MASSA 03
Zhu

▲ POLIS MASSA INTERIOR
Jaeger

◀ POLIS MASSA 01
Jaeger

◀ DROID GENERAL 01
Fu

"Darth Vader is black, so I went with pure white. In the Chinese culture, white means death."—Fu

▶ WINGED GENERAL
McCaig

A NEW ICON OF EVIL

NOVEMBER 9–15, 2002

On November 8, Lucas announces that Episode III will have a new villain: the general of the Separatist droid armies. He says that it could be part alien or droid, but that it has to read immediately as an enemy. For November 15, with the exception of Church, the entire art department gives the concept a shot. While no one scores an immediate success, Lucas does think some of the droid concepts are working and asks to see more.

◀ DROID GENERAL 02 (INSET)
Fu

▲ DROID GENERAL 01
Thompson

▲ GENERAL 04
Thompson

"This had started out with an open mouth, screaming—but it freaked me out, so I painted over it."—TIEMENS

▼ WIDE ALIEN GENERAL
Tiemens

▲ GENERAL 03
Thompson

▲ GENERAL 02
Thompson

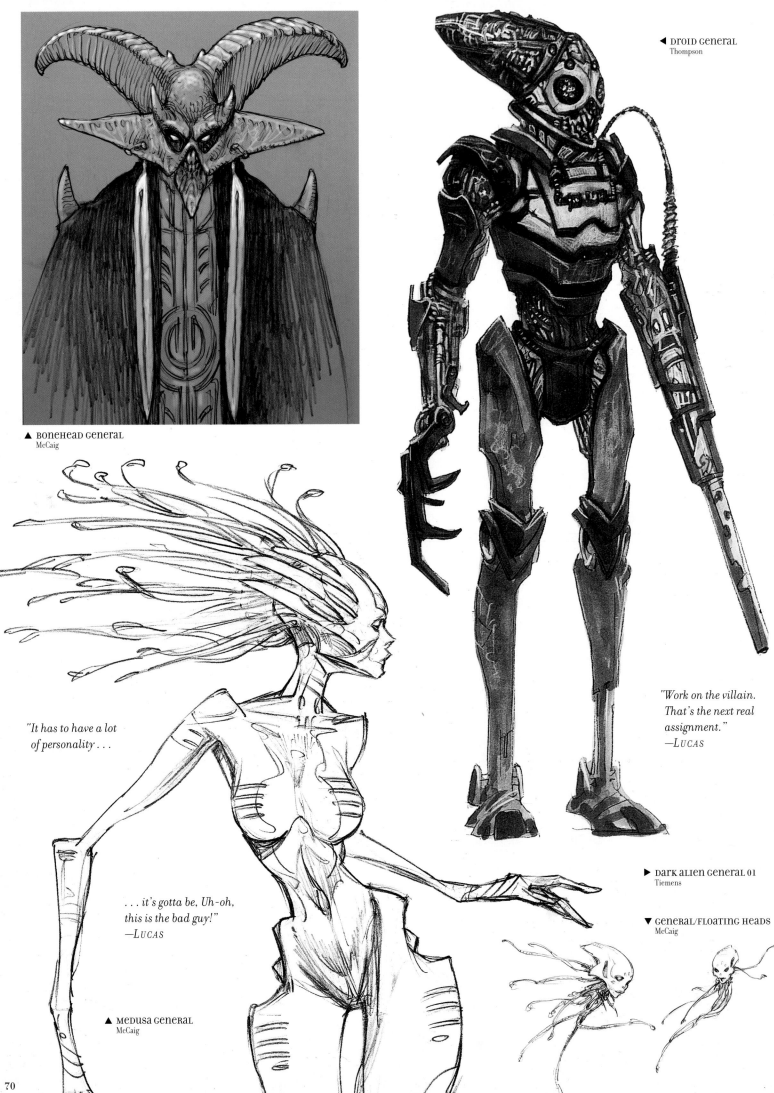

▲ BONEHEAD GENERAL
McCaig

◄ DROID GENERAL
Thompson

*"It has to have a lot
of personality . . .*

*. . . it's gotta be, Uh-oh,
this is the bad guy!"*
—LUCAS

▲ MEDUSA GENERAL
McCaig

*"Work on the villain.
That's the next real
assignment."*
—LUCAS

▶ DARK ALIEN GENERAL 01
Tiemens

▼ GENERAL/FLOATING HEADS
McCaig

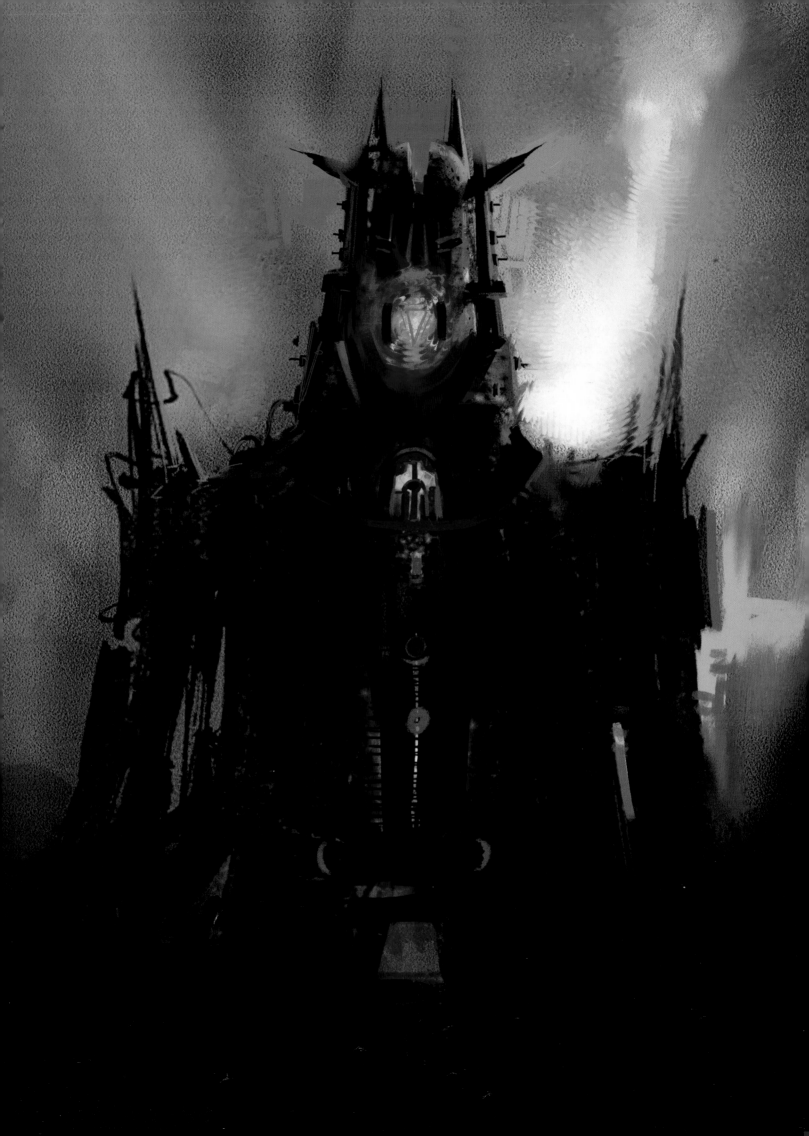

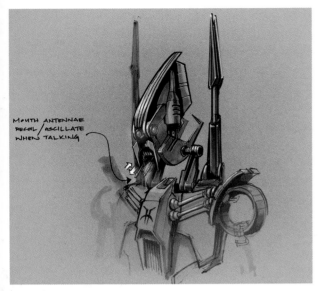

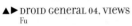
MOUTH ANTENNAE RECOIL / OSCILLATE WHEN TALKING

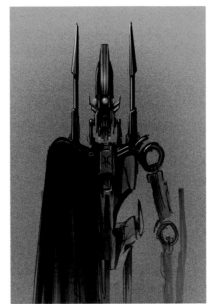

▲▶ DROID GENERAL 04, VIEWS
Fu

▲ DROID GENERAL GUARDS
Fu

▲ "THE GENERAL" DROID
Jaeger

▼ "THE GENERAL" 01
Jaeger

"The head of what became the general's droid guard is actually the back of a spray nozzle. I was just trying to carry on the Star Wars tradition of taking pieces of junk and turning them into something."—FU

"We had nothing to go on, except he was evil and dark."—JAEGER

▶ DARK ALIEN GENERAL 02
Tiemens

▲ CORUSCANT LOVE DECK
Tiemens

"I looked a lot at Gérôme
[Jean Léon, 1824-1904],
the Pre-Raphaelite painters,
and the Orientalists, so
you have that exotic mix
of costumes and lighting."
—TIEMENS

"I was also inspired by the work of Sir
Lawrence Alma-Tadema [1836-1912], a
Dutch painter who influenced the look of
D. W. Griffith's films."—TIEMENS

◄ PADMÉ'S VERANDA—WIDE 01 & 02
Tiemens

▲ LOVE ALCOVE ON CORUSCANT
Tiemens

At the November 22 and December 6 meetings, the design direction for the Separatist general is chosen and honed. Lucas also finalizes the direction for the droid's henchmen. On December 13, Lucas approves the eyes and sockets. The following Friday, he approves the character's full body design. The artists also present possibilities for his vehicle. Last but not least, as Lucas nears completion of his rough draft of the script, he gives the general a name: Grievous.

◄ DROID GENERAL, RED ROBE (INSET)
Fu

"George went right up to this drawing [below] and said, 'That's the one.' I mentioned that the general might have organic eyes, and he said, 'Now that's interesting.'"—FU

▲ DROID GENERAL
Fu

"All the guys were saying, 'Wouldn't it be cool if Grievous's shield was made out of the only material that deflects lightsabers [right]?'"—FU

◄ DROID GENERAL, RED ROBE (INSET)
Fu

◄ DROID GENERAL, SAMURAI (INSET)
Fu

◄ DARTH VADER IN *A NEW HOPE* (INSET)

"By putting the general's henchmen behind him [left], he stands out as the leader. This harks back to the image of Darth Vader appearing for the first time backed by the stormtroopers."—FU

▲ GENERAL, ORGANIC EYES
Fu

► GENERAL WITH WEAPONS
Fu

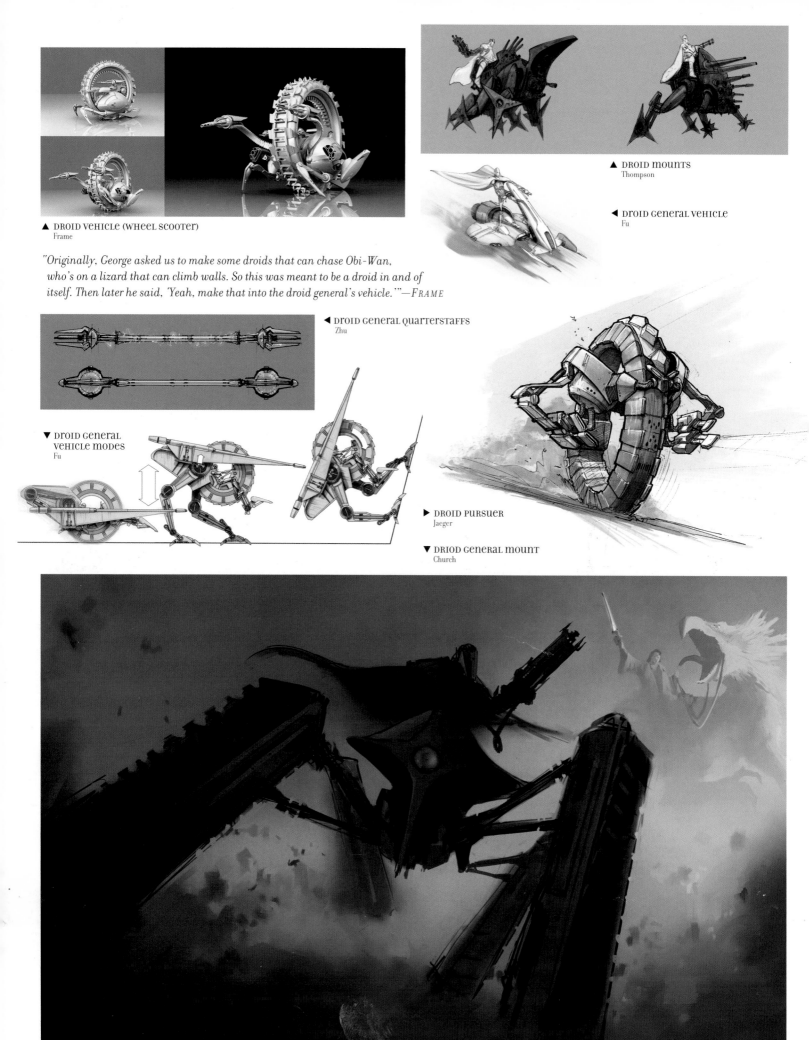

▲ DROID VEHICLE (WHEEL SCOOTER)
Frame

▲ DROID MOUNTS
Thompson

◀ DROID GENERAL VEHICLE
Fu

"Originally, George asked us to make some droids that can chase Obi-Wan, who's on a lizard that can climb walls. So this was meant to be a droid in and of itself. Then later he said, 'Yeah, make that into the droid general's vehicle.'"—FRAME

◀ DROID GENERAL QUARTERSTAFFS
Zhu

▼ DROID GENERAL VEHICLE MODES
Fu

▶ DROID PURSUER
Jaeger

▼ DRIOD GENERAL MOUNT
Church

▶ **JEDI COSTUME CONCEPT**
McCaig

▲ **YODA CONCEPT 01**
Jun

DECEMBER 13–20, 2002

For years, the Clone Wars have been raging, and they've taken their toll on the thinly spread Jedi. Jun creates a sullen Yoda, McCaig imagines a blinded Eeth Koth, and Thompson imagines Ki-Adi-Mundi with one eye less. "I did battle armor for Plo Koon," Thompson says, "and tried a lightsaber that was attached to his wrist. George said, 'I don't know about this,' but stamped it okay for the costume."

"By the third film, you have a lot of characters left over from before, and they're all running around yipping and yelling and saying, 'What about me?'"—LUCAS, ON WRITING THE SCRIPT

▼ **EETH KOTH & MACE WINDU**
McCaig

▲ **JEDI WARRIOR CONCEPT**
Dahlslett

▲ **PLO KOON BATTLE DRESS**
Thompson

▲ **KI-ADI-MUNDI BATTLE DRESS**
Thompson

81

▶ PADMÉ 02
Jun

*"The red is in her hair
because it's the end of
the film, and I thought
she might be going after
the bull [Anakin]."*
—MCCAIG

◀ PADMÉ 09
McCaig

◀ PADMÉ ON MUSTAFAR
McCaig

▲ PADMÉ COSTUME
CONCEPT 01
McCaig

▶ PADMÉ COSTUME
CONCEPT 04
McCaig

DECEMBER 13–20, 2002

One question that persists throughout much of early preproduction is how much to show of Padmé's pregnant condition. Whether she would give birth during the film wasn't known, so various costume designs are proposed. Eventually, Lucas decides that her clothes have to make it subtly clear to audiences that she is "expecting" without having her pregnancy become a source of distraction.

▲ PADMÉ HEADDRESS 07
McCaig

"George wanted the costumes to hide the fact that she's pregnant, because she's concealing it from others."
—JUN

▲ PADMÉ HAIR CONCEPT 02
McCaig

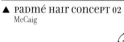

▲ PADMÉ COSTUME CONCEPT 09
Jun

▶ PADMÉ PREGNANT 08
McCaig

▶ PADMÉ 06
McCaig

◀ PADMÉ 03
Jun

▲ anakin and padmé
McCaig

"I wanted to show that this poor guy is trapped by shadows, and she's stuck in the light. And the hand that reaches out to touch her isn't even a human hand anymore."—McCaig

star-crossed lover wars

December 13–20, 2002

On December 13, 2002, Lucas acknowledges that Queen Organa—Senator Bail Organa's wife, who would come to raise Leia Skywalker—will appear in the film. He also stipulates that she is in her midthirties, peaceful, and trustworthy. Meanwhile, because the script is still being written, the artists are still free to imagine what might happen in the course of the film. A great deal of time is spent speculating on the events surrounding Padmé and her eventual fate . . . "I was brainstorming with Iain," Tiemens says, "and he thought Padmé might have a dagger in her hand. George responded favorably and said, 'I'm starting to see some scenes . . .'"

▲ queen organa with padmé
McCaig

▲ queen organa
McCaig

"It's the spirit of my wife [above], everything I love about being in love with my wife, Leonor. It's the thing I love drawing more than anything else in the world."— McCaig

◀ padmé carrying twins
McCaig

"I thought that Queen Organa [above] might look almost exactly like Padmé, because Leia remembers seeing her mother smile."—McCaig

▲ PADMÉ WITH DAGGER
McCaig

"George wanted to see Anakin in a costume similar to the one that Luke wears in Return of the Jedi.*"—JUN*

▲ ANAKIN COSTUME
CONCEPT 01
Jun

▲ BAIL ORGANA COSTUME CONCEPT 01
Jun

▲ DARK PADMÉ
Tiemens

"The moment Padmé realizes Anakin can't be saved, she should do the thing that she needs to do—out of love. She should kill him."—MCCAIG

▲ ANAKIN COSTUME
CONCEPT 03
Jun

▲ ANAKIN AND PADMÉ ON MUSTAFAR
Tiemens

▲ FELUCIA FOREST
Church

*"George wanted to combine a bunch of Felucia
sketches, so I did these two [forest and desert]."*
—CHURCH

▲ CLONE WAR KEY FRAME
Thompson

*"This was all pre-script still. This is the Padawan
younglings being forced to fight. And we thought
it might be cool, since they can't fight all alone,
if they fought in formation in order to face off
against the droids—but they'd still be slain."*
—THOMPSON

◄ FELUCIA KEY FRAME
Jun

A CHASE IS ANNOUNCED

DECEMBER 13–20, 2002

In addition to re-presenting the "kelp planet,"
Felucia, with all the previous concepts combined
into one, the artists—joined by prequel veteran
Michael Murnane—continue to suggest battle
scenes. The lizard hasn't yet been assigned to a
planet, so Church puts him on Saleucami, the
bridge world—at which point, on December 13,
2002, Lucas confirms that the lizard will be seen
on Utapau. He adds that there will be a big chase
on that planet, with Obi-Wan pursuing the evil
droid general Grievous.

▲ FELUCIA DESERT
Church

MORE MUSTAFAR DUELING

DECEMBER 13–20, 2002

Responding to the needs of the script, artists
create a conference room on the planet
Mustafar, where Anakin confronts the
Separatist council. For the volcano planet,
Lucas asks that the architecture be built near
and around lava flows so there is always
a heightened sense of danger.

▶ MUSTAFAR CONFERENCE ROOM
Church

▼ LANDSCAPE WITH GREEN SKY (AND "JUN" BUG)
Tiemens

▲ PLATFORMS
Jaeger

▶ MUSTAFAR CATWALK
Fu

"I had in mind the catwalk scene from The Empire Strikes Back, *when Luke is out there and the wind is blowing.* Star Wars *is all about dangerous catwalks."*—FU

▼LAVA LEDGE & RED SEA (INSETS)
Tiemens

▲ FAMILY PORTRAIT
McCaig

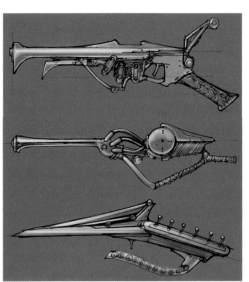

▲ WOOKIEE BLASTERS
Zhu

"It's not in the script anymore, but we were told that Han Solo was on Kashyyyk and that he was being raised by Chewbacca. He's such a persnickety guy later on—he always has to have the best of everything—so I thought it'd be great if when he was a kid, he was an absolute slob."
—McCaig

HAN SOLO

Lucas asks for a conference room on Kashyyyk—and a costume for a young Han Solo, who is slated to meet Yoda on this planet and actually help him to locate general Grievous. His one and only costume and character style are approved as soon as they're presented.

► WOOKIEE
CONCEPT 05
Jun

▼ WOOKIEE LINEUP
Jun

▼ CONFERENCE ROOM 04
Church

"We found out that Yoda is on Kashyyyk, and that he fights clone troopers and takes a lot of them out."—Zhu

▲ HAN SOLO
McCaig

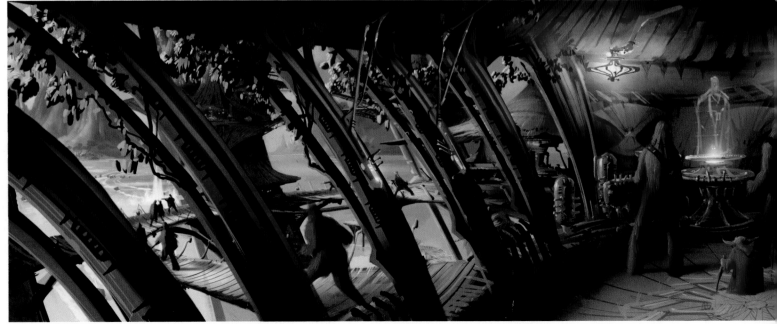

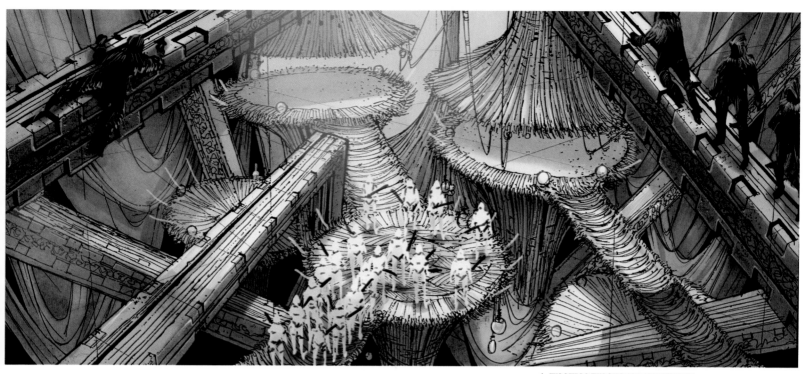

THE MUSTAFAR-UTAPAU CONNECTION

JANUARY 10–31, 2003

Although the red-cloaked, mummified creatures were originally designed for Mustafar, Lucas decides to move them to Utapau. The former Utapauns, the lemur people, are thus temporarily discarded, deleted from the film. Lucas also describes a sequence where Obi-Wan is wounded and falls into one of the sinkholes, where he meets a cave monster. "I thought the monster was a symbolic threshold guardian," McCaig says, "guarding the secret of how you come back from death—not literally, but metaphorically, because the treasure is Qui-Gon Jinn."

▲ MUSTAFAR/UTAPAU MALE & FEMALE
(MICHAEL MURNANE & FAY DAVID)
McCaig

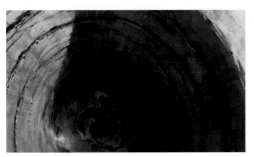

▲ DEEP SINKHOLE 01
Tiemens

▲ CLIFF & ALIENS (UTAPAU)
Tiemens

◄ CAVE MONSTER 01
McCaig

► MUSTAFAR/UTAPAU
MALE SCULPT
Murnane

▼ MUSTAFAR/UTAPAU
FEMALE SCULPT
Barnes

◀ SINKHOLE GROTTO (OBI-WAN & QUI-GON)
Tiemens

"Iain said, 'Wouldn't it be great to see an apparition of Qui-Gon while Obi's down there in the cave, giving him guidance?' The painting wasn't used in the story, though."—TIEMENS

◀ UTAPAU TUNNEL
Zhu

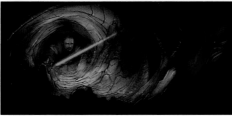

"This was approved a couple times for the Utapau sequence where we thought Ki-Adi-Mundi might be riding it. So I quickly did a small one like this just to get the proportions, which took two or three days."
—MICHAEL PATRICK MURNANE

▲ SINKHOLE GROTTO
Tiemens

◀ UTAPAU MONSTER
McCaig

▶ DACTILLION SCULPTURE
Murnane

"I was hoping that Grievous's vehicle was sentient, or that Grievous would plug into it and make it sentient. It's really a moment about eye contact between adversaries."—CHURCH

▲ OBI-WAN/GENERAL GRIEVOUS FACE-OFF
Church

Upon seeing several early renderings of the general's quarters, Lucas requests that the artists add two control panels, like those in the Emperor's throne room in *Return of the Jedi*. After it goes through a few permutations, Lucas approves the "general's quarters" (aka "admiral's/captain's quarters" and "throne room"). These designs are immediately sent to Bocquet, as are those for the ship's bridge, so blueprints can be drawn up.

▲ CAPTAIN'S QUARTERS, SEPARATIST CRUISER
Church

◀ BIRD'S EYE II (GENERAL'S QUARTERS)
Frame

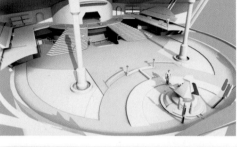
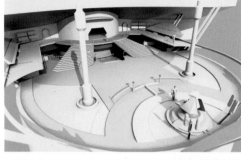

"Near the end of preproduction—when George would approve two drawings, or parts of drawings—T. J. [Frame] would model them together; then all we had to do was paint on top of them."—CHURCH

▼ CRUISER CRASH
Church

▶ BRIDGE DETAIL
Fu & Frame

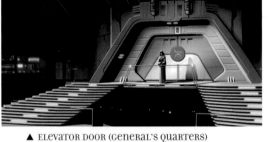

▲ ELEVATOR DOOR (GENERAL'S QUARTERS)
Fu

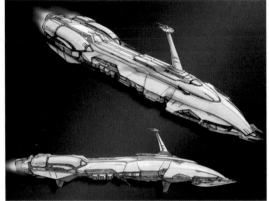

▲ DROID GENERAL SHIP
Jaeger

"I tried to incorporate some of the droid general's features into the ship. The tower is where the throne room is, and the elevator shaft is inside that tower."—JAEGER

▲ BIRD'S EYE (GENERAL'S QUARTERS), REVISED
Fu

▶ PALPATINE'S
COSTUME 03
McCaig

▶ MAS AMEDDA
Jun

JANUARY 10–31, 2003

Lucas makes it clear, as of January 10, that one of the last shots of the film will take place on an Imperial Star Destroyer. The artists therefore undertake the creation of early Imperial officer uniforms. In addition, the one and only new concept painting for Grand Moff Tarkin—played by Peter Cushing in A *New Hope*—is approved on January 17. The artists also learn of Episode III's title: *Revenge of the Sith*.

▼ PALPATINE'S ANTECHAMBER, REVISED
Church

"Parts of the early antechamber [below] were incorporated into what became Palpatine's office."—CHURCH

▼ PALPATINE'S ANTECHAMBER
Church

▶ palpatine
costume
concept 01
McCaig

...and chambers

JANUARY 10–31, 2003

Lucas asks for modifications to Palpatine's antechamber, incorporating narrower bench seating and two small chairs. Because the script contains a few scenes for this area, Lucas approves construction of the entire Palpatine office/antechamber set on January 24. He reveals that it may be here that Anakin succumbs to the dark side.

▶ grand moff tarkin
McCaig

▲ imperial officers 01
Jun

▼ palpatine's
antechamber
Fu

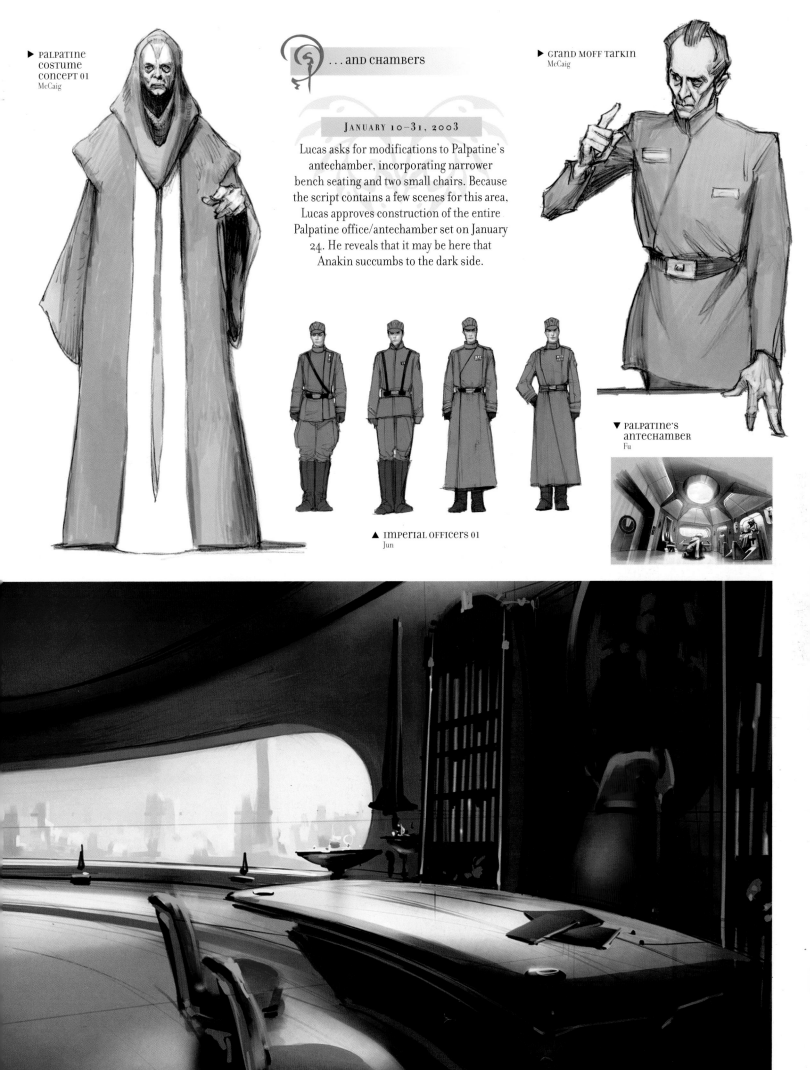

"This kind of pushed George's barrier on loose painting. It could be an abandoned tower where some kind of evil droid is creating Vader." —TIEMENS

THE DARK TOWER OF THE SITH

JANUARY 10–31, 2003

At the January 10 meeting, Lucas also tells the artists he'll need a room where Anakin is reassembled after his near-fatal duel with Obi-Wan Kenobi. It is here that he'll be transformed into the Darth Vader of the 1977 *Star Wars* film.

At the following gathering, Lucas approves designs for an establishing shot and a reverse angle, but specifies that the room needs to be big enough for medical droids to move around in.

▲ REHAB ROOM 01
Tiemens

"This was something I'd been thinking about my entire life—the moment the lid goes on Darth Vader. The room is scary, like a dentist's office. Very much later, I found out that Darth Vader freaks out in here." —CHURCH

▶ REHAB ROOM 06
Tiemens

▼ VADER CHAMBER 02
Church

▼▶ REHAB ROOM 03 (INSET)
Tiemens

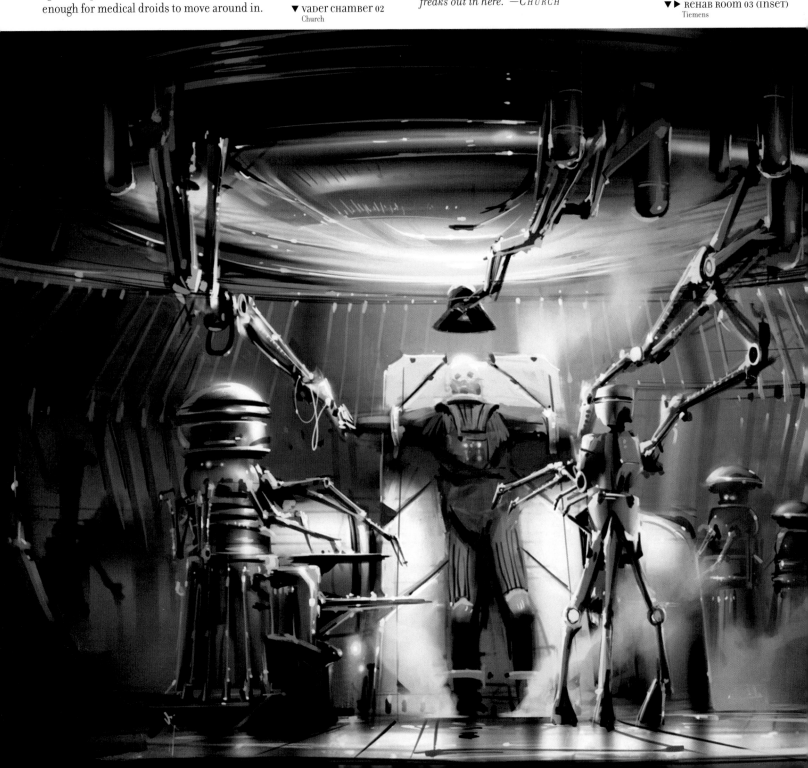

FEBRUARY 7–21, 2003

On January 31, the day the rough draft is typed up, Lucas informs the artists that he'll need concepts for a funeral scene on Naboo. The first "horses" designed to pull Padmé's casket are too much like the Earth animal, so Lucas suggests something more like the kaadus—the Gungan steeds—from *The Phantom Menace*. At first, he considers shooting the funeral crowd scenes on Isola Bella, an island in Italy, but later opts for a digital set; only certain elements will be filmed during principal photography in Sydney—which is only months away.

▶ HORSE
creatures
Jun

▲ PADMÉ FUNERAL COSTUME
McCaig

"This is my favorite painting that I've ever done for the whole prequel trilogy. I was there when Padmé was born as a character, and now I was burying her. The flowers are tears."—MCCAIG

▲ AERIAL SPACE BATTLE
Church

▶ SEPARATIST CRUISER MODEL
Goodson

BATTLE OVER CORUSCANT

FEBRUARY 7–28, 2003

While Lucas continues to approve paintings for various sequences aboard the Trade Federation cruiser and during the aerial dogfight, he says that some scenes may change as he proceeds through the first draft of the script. He also requests that fewer towers be visible on the Coruscant crash site.

"In the beginning, Ryan was pushing towards more of a Mygeeto, crystal-world look for the cruiser. But George kept saying it had to look like a spaceship and not like a glass ship, so we started doing more of a traditional industrial Star Wars look."—FU

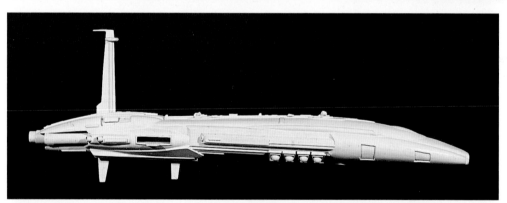

▶ VERTICAL EXPLOSIONS
Tiemens

108

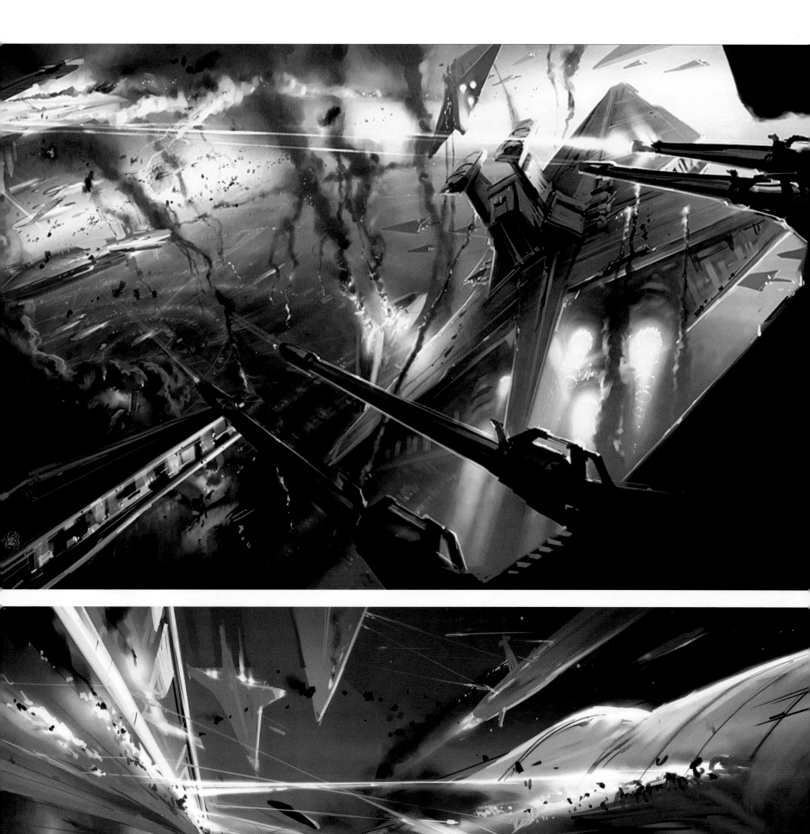

▲ CAPITAL SHIP EXCHANGE
Church

▲ JEDI IN FLIGHT
Church

▼ CORUSCANT CRASH
Church

▲ JEDI GAG (WHAT'S BEHIND DOOR NUMBER 1?)
Zhu

"You might want to play with the ship pulling apart . . . When the ship crashes, there can be fireships pouring foam on it."—LUCAS

► coruscant cruiser crash
Zhu

▲ coruscant cruiser crash site
Zhu

"George said the fireships looked too much like submarines, so I removed the conning towers. We used red and white for high visibility."—CHURCH

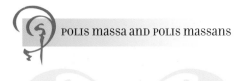

▲ LANDING 01
Zhu

FEBRUARY 7–28, 2003

After reviewing various concepts for the Polis Massans, Lucas okays different body types and faceplates, and the way in which they utilize hand gestures to communicate. He suggests, however, that the artists do more work on the faceplate texture. Ultimately, dolphin skin is studied as source material. For the medical center, Church uses blue-green shades, noting that Soviet psychologists found them to be the most soothing colors.

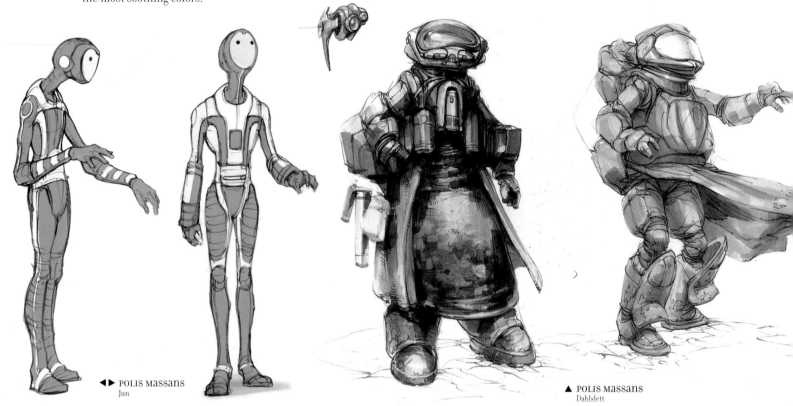

◀▶ POLIS MASSANS
Jun

▲ POLIS MASSANS
Dahlslett

▲ POLIS MASSA LANDING AREA
Zhu

112

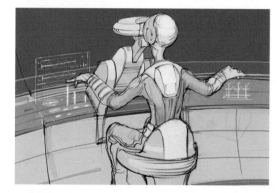

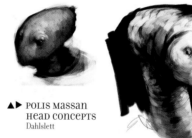

▲ MEDICAL CENTER 01
Zhu

▲▶ POLIS MASSAN
HEAD CONCEPTS
Dahlslett

◀ POLIS MASSAN AT WORK
Jun

▼ POLIS MASSAN MEDICAL CENTER
Church

"George told us that this is where the twins
are born—and Padmé dies. We knew we'd be
crosscutting to Darth Vader's [rehabilitation]
chamber, so I wanted to make this one [below]
the opposite of that."—CHURCH

FEBRUARY 28, 2003

As the animatics department is about to begin creating 3-D digital storyboards, more traditional storyboards are needed to help in the development of videomatics, because film editor Ben Burtt will use both 3-D and 2-D storyboards to create this film-before-the-film. Thus Thompson, McCaig, and Jun begin drawing. "We had an outline," Thompson says. "We knew the opening sequence was an Indiana Jones thing on a spaceship. Beyond that, the ideas came out of the storyboarding process. We had a great first meeting with Ben and just started hammering it out. The early boards were done very crudely to cover a huge amount of action; we were all drawing in rudimentary form 'beats'—the key moments." When Lucas reviews these first storyboards, an impromptu brainstorming session occurs in the art department, and scenes begin to take form.

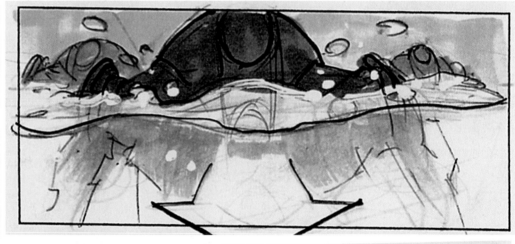

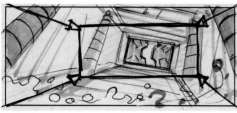

▲ SEPARATIST CRUISER ACTION STORYBOARDS
Thompson

"The real call to begin was when Ben [Burtt] started on videomatics and we needed to give him something to start editing with—and to help George start seeing on paper what ideas were working out and what wasn't."
—THOMPSON

GENERAL GRIEVOUS

MARCH 14, 2003

After weeks of preparation, Robert Barnes unveils his General Grievous sculpt. Lucas approves it and adds an "organ sac" to house the droid's vitals—his guts, which, except for his eyes, are the general's only other organic parts. Lucas also asks for more greeblie wires in the arms, and a spinal cord that goes from the droid's neck to the organ sac, which should be covered by metal plating. "For the Grievous sculpt, my approach was to keep in mind the character first, followed by design, then function. So I spent a week building just the armature. Ryan decided we should explore more design for the rest of the body. He did some quick studies and consulted with Jun and Iain. We stuck everyone's favorite parts into the sculpture, with the idea that Grievous is an elite droid, so he wouldn't have anything reminiscent of standard droids. I came up with opposing split arms, because of the way the forms were developing."

▶ GENERAL GRIEVOUS SCULPTURE
Barnes

"Whatever I was designing had to look right and be mechanically right, and work in CG."
—BARNES

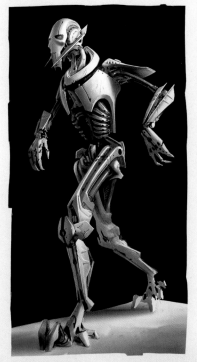

▲ DROID GENERAL
REVISION (BODY)
Church

▲ DROID GENERAL COLORS
Church

115

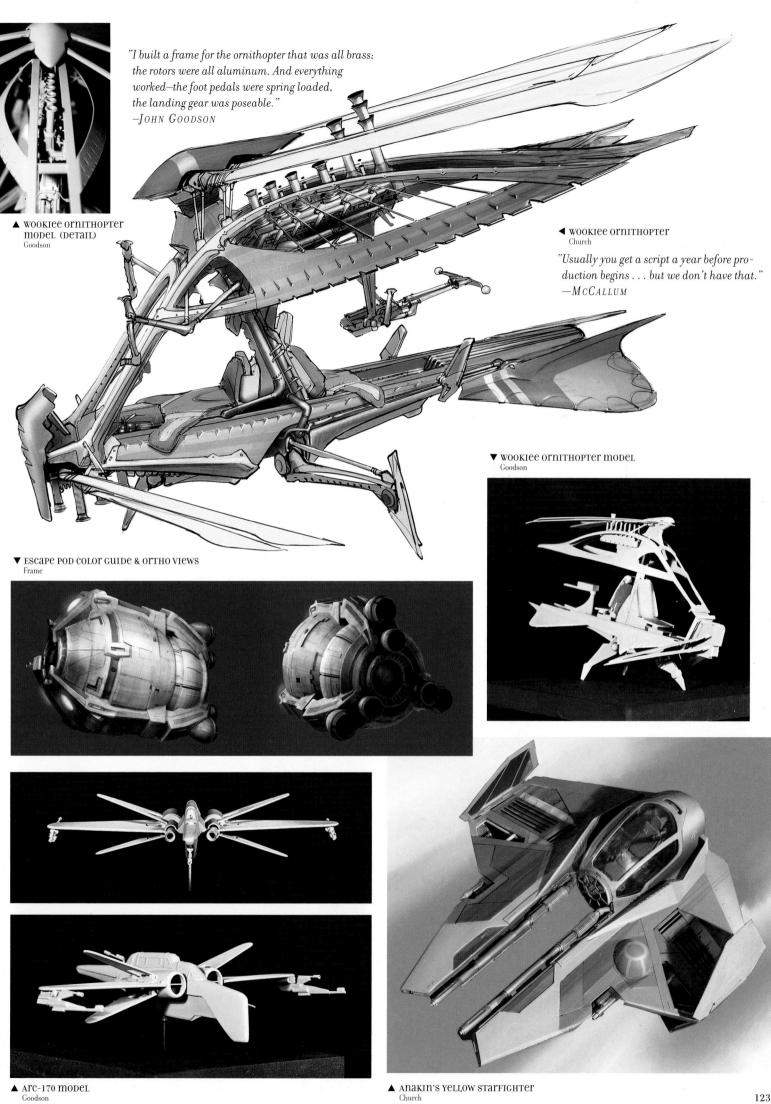

▲ wookiee ornithopter model (detail)
Goodson

"I built a frame for the ornithopter that was all brass; the rotors were all aluminum. And everything worked—the foot pedals were spring loaded, the landing gear was poseable."
—JOHN GOODSON

◄ wookiee ornithopter
Church

"Usually you get a script a year before production begins . . . but we don't have that."
—McCALLUM

▼ wookiee ornithopter model
Goodson

▼ escape pod color guide & ortho views
Frame

▲ arc-170 model
Goodson

▲ anakin's yellow starfighter
Church

123

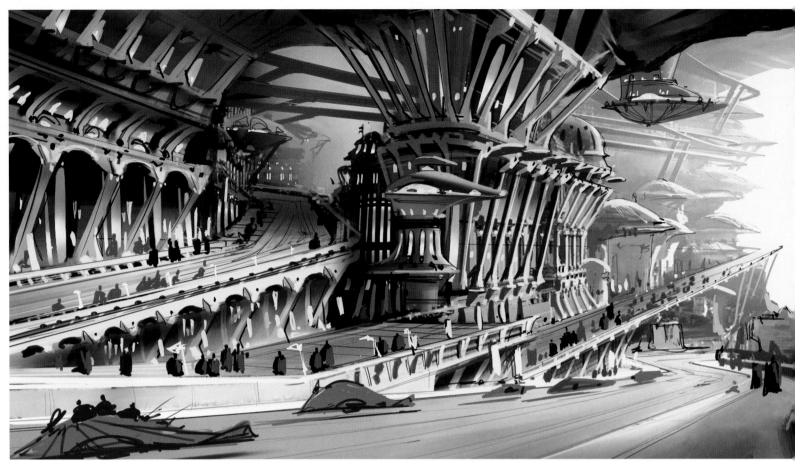

▲ UTAPAU CITY, MULTILEVEL
Church

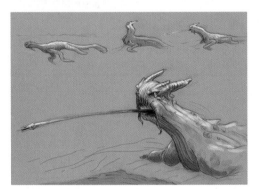

▲ GROTTO MONSTER TONGUE
Murnane

▲ UTAPAU INTERIOR
Zhu

▲ GROTTO MONSTER
Murnane

TEXTURING UTAPAU

APRIL 4–25, 2003

On April 4, Lucas asks to see much more of the Utapau interiors—its businesses and living spaces—and requests that it be more high-tech. At the same time, the lizard's color is conditionally approved, as long as it looks good when compared to the colors used for the completed sinkhole. On April 11, 2003, many more designs are presented to Lucas, and the look of the Utapau interiors is finalized. He also approves the cave monster design, requesting that its eyes be made larger. As the look of Utapau progresses, newcomer Danny Wagner is brought aboard to sculpt 3-D environments.

▼ GROTTO MONSTER
McCaig

► CHASE (WITH PLANTS),
FRAME 04
Tiemens

▲ REVISED UTAPAU SINKHOLE, SCULPTURE
Wagner

"I built it out of plywood, Y2-Klay, and other materials, and gave it a very cracked look. I added a little operation building with antennas from one of Erik [Tiemen's] paintings. Then I painted it with gouache and used some chalk to enhance the surface treatment."—*DANNY WAGNER*

▼ UPPER LANDSCAPE 01
Tiemens

▲ UPPER LANDSCAPE 02
Tiemens

"I'd been pushing for this savanna look. The 'sentinels' were inspired by Ralph McQuarrie."—*TIEMENS*

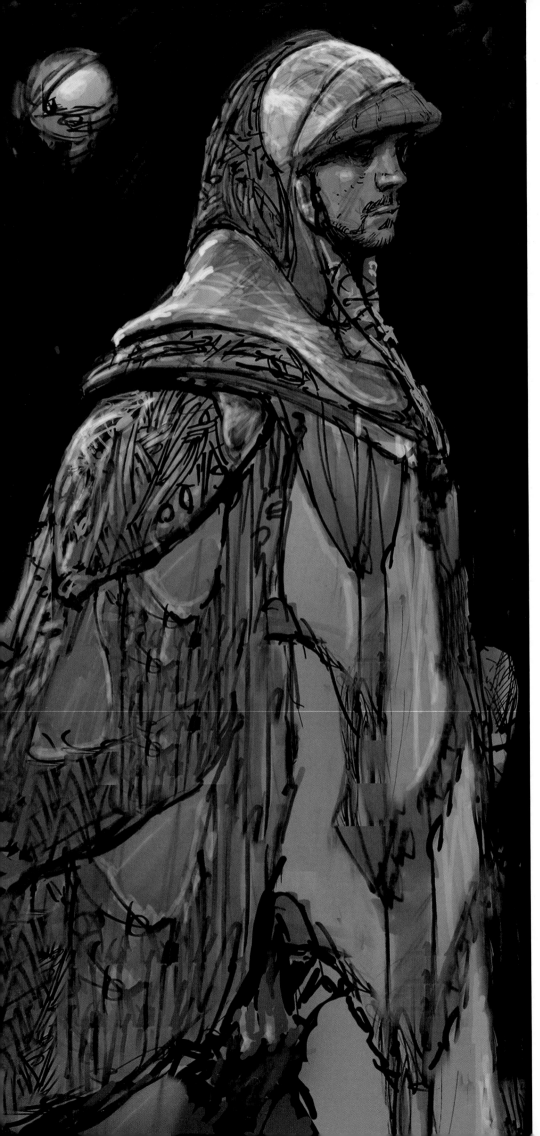

▲ senator costume concepts
McCaig

▲ senator concepts 01
McCaig

▲ orn free taa & senator costume concepts
Jun

◄ bail organa costume concept
McCaig

▲ palpatine costume concepts
Dahlslett

▲ YOUNG JEDI COSTUME CONCEPT
(JETT LUCAS)
Jun

▲ SENATOR COSTUME
CONCEPT
Dahlslett

▲ MYSTIC SENATOR 02
McCaig

▲ MYSTIC SENATOR CONCEPT (KATIE LUCAS)
McCaig

CRITICAL COSTUMES

APRIL 11-25, 2003

Having finished his first draft on April 10, 2003, Lucas holds a crucial meeting with costume designer Trisha Biggar, much of which is devoted to discussion of Senatorial outfits. Lucas specifies that he'll need four costumes for women—Mon Mothma, two Senators to be played by Lucas's daughters (Amanda and Katie), and a fourth—along with four for men, whose identities will be determined later. In addition, a Jedi costume is needed for Lucas's son, Jett.

◀▼ PALPATINE COSTUME
CONCEPTS
Jun

▲ SENATOR COSTUME CONCEPT (AMANDA LUCAS)
McCaig

127

▼▶ CLONE TROOPER, KNEELING AND STANDING
Jun

▼ CLONE TROOPER, VIEWS
Jun

▲ NEIMOIDIAN SOLDIER
Jun

▲ ALIEN SOLDIER CONCEPT
Thompson

"Everything in the Star Wars universe has to be built. There's no place you can go and rent a Star Wars prop—it's just a different kind of filmmaking." —MCCALLUM

▲ NEIMOIDIAN SOLDIER, HEAD
Jun

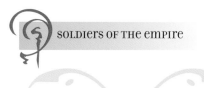

With Neimoidians scattered throughout the prequel trilogy, Lucas decides to create a new type for *Revenge of the Sith*: a Neimoidian trooper. He opts to convert four preexisting pilot masks into soldiers, and approves the construction of six costumes. While clone troopers also receive new garbs, Vader's operating table and medical capsule are conceptually begun—the latter designed to transport Anakin's maimed body from Mustafar to Coruscant.

▲ vader room 3d render
Frame

▲ rehabilitation chamber
Frame

"[Anakin's] rationalization is: 'Everybody is after power. Even the Jedi are after power.' Therefore, he thinks, 'They're all equally corrupt now. So which side am I going to be on? Do I align myself with Palpatine, who is a Sith Lord and who can possibly help me save Padmé? Or do I side with the Jedi and maybe lose Padmé?'"—LUCAS

▲ darth vader on operating table
Church

▲ anakin's med capsule (for carrying the near-death figure)
Church

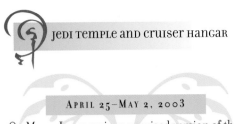

JEDI TEMPLE AND CRUISER HANGAR

APRIL 25–MAY 2, 2003

On May 1, Lucas reviews a revised version of the
Jedi Temple circuit room and approves the larger
space. It's here that Obi-Wan will disconnect a
trap designed to snare errant Jedi. In fact, in
Episode III, the Jedi Temple will suffer a lethal
attack, so other designs are needed to show
the extent of the damage.

*"We wanted to make all of our hangar spaces—
all our generic spaces—very cluttered. I always
tell the guys to look at the hangar in* Empire
*[below, inset], where there's junk everywhere
—and it looks awesome."*—CHURCH

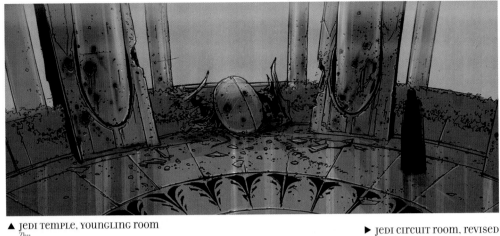

▲ JEDI TEMPLE, YOUNGLING ROOM
Zhu

▶ JEDI CIRCUIT ROOM, REVISED
Church

*"George liked the idea that it looked like
circuitry [left], but he wanted a much
bigger space [right]. I imagine these big
things being able to move like stacks in
a library."*—CHURCH

◀ JEDI CIRCUIT ROOM
Church

▼ JEDI CRUISER HANGAR
Church

JEDI TEMPLE - CIRCUIT ROOM
RYAN CHURCH
16 MAY 03
RVS

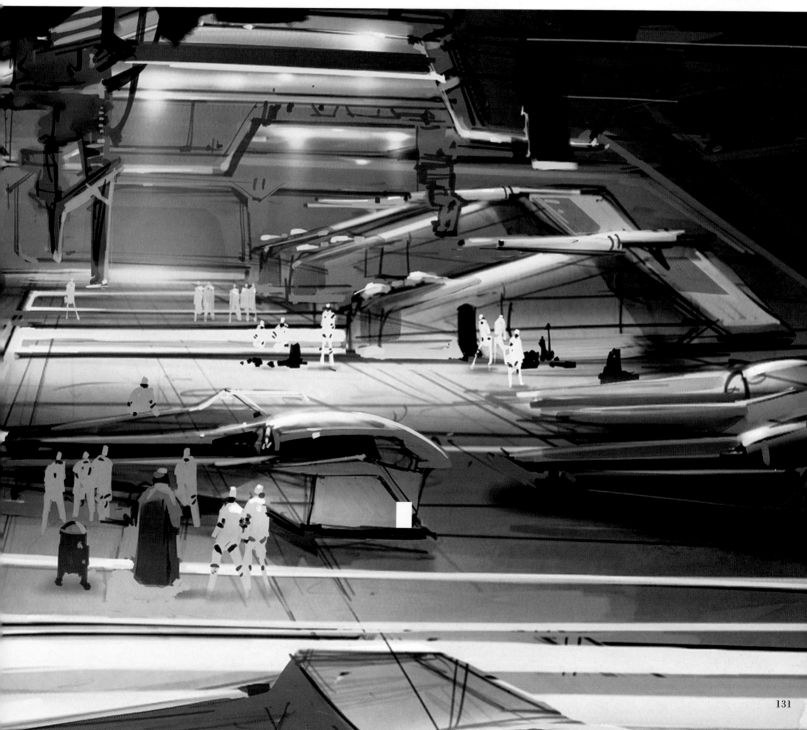

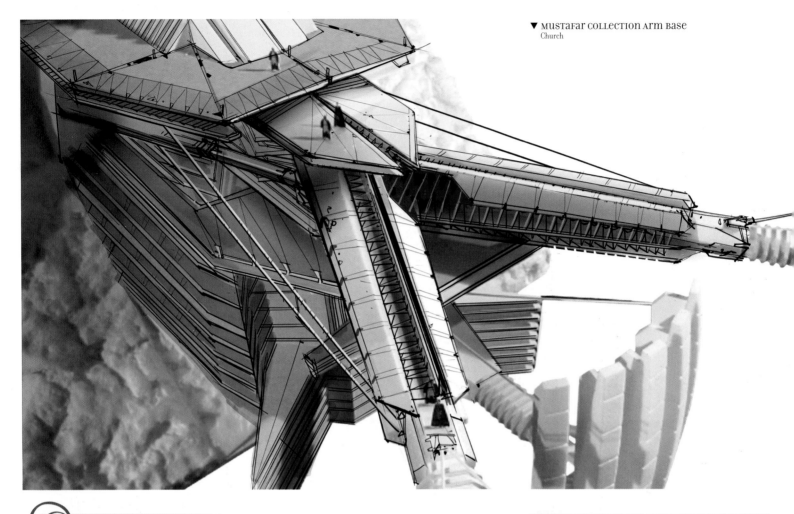

FALL-OF-VADER, TAKE 1

MAY 2–23, 2003

The first draft of the script states that Obi-Wan maims Anakin at the end of their duel on Mustafar, so Lucas asks for visuals that show possible expositions. Production also needs to know more about the specifics of the duel and the locales. Toward those ends, Thompson presents one possible interpretation of the scene, while others work on the look of the "collection arms," and their relation to the volcanic environment.

"Gavin [Bouquet] calls. He needs to know how much set to build on Mustafar. Fay calls: We're going to board this whole sequence out. I think, Great, we're going to board the big swordfight— so we just jump in!"—THOMPSON

▼ THE CLIMACTIC DUAL STORYBOARDS
Thompson

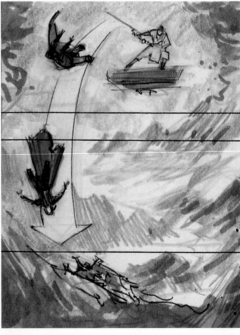

▲ MUSTAFAR BALCONY
Church

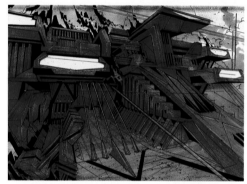

▼ MUSTAFAR FLOATING BATTLE
Church

▲ MUSTAFAR BUNKER DETAILS
Zhu

▶ PADMÉ HAIR 03
McCaig

▶ HANDMAIDEN COSTUME
Jun

▲ PADMÉ HAIR 04
McCaig

COIFFURES OF PADMÉ

MAY 2–30, 2003

Lucas asks the artists to design an area on Alderaan where the infant Leia will be given to Queen Organa. Upon seeing the balcony shown in an early illustration, he asks for a revision that has the seat built into the sidewall, and Queen Organa sitting at more of an angle. With Padmé's costumes fairly fixed, attention turns to her hair. Jun and McCaig come up with a number of arrangements for Lucas to choose from. None are approved as is, but combinations are okayed.

◀ PADMÉ HAIR CONCEPT 01
Jun

◀ PADMÉ WITH BLASTER, HAIR CONCEPT 03
McCaig

▲ PADMÉ WRAP
McCaig

▲ ALDERAAN BALCONY INTERIOR, REVISED
Church

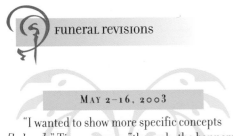

funeral revisions

"I wanted to show more specific concepts [below]," Tiemens says, "the arch, the banners, little wedges of light, along with glowing lights. We went for a predawn look—and Jun had just designed these great horses."

▶ FUNERAL PROCESSION
Jun

"Through the portrayal of light, I wanted to imply that she's going to heaven."—JUN

▼ NABOO FUNERAL
Tiemens

▲ padmé as coruscant burns
Tiemens

▼ palpatine reveal, lighting
Tiemens

shades of destruction

may 16–30, 2003

Following art department procedure after a
design is fixed, Tiemens works on color passes,
so that different combinations can be tested.
Because digital filmmaking gives the director
more freedom than ever before, Lucas has
decided that the film's skies and time
sequences will follow a detailed choreography,
with storms beginning in one scene, deepening
in the next, and erupting in another.

▲ general's quarters (throne room) lighting
Tiemens

nightmare droids—and more

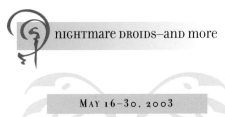

MAY 16–30, 2003

Throughout the *Star Wars* saga, droids often act as nurses and doctors. Following in that tradition, Lucas asks Church to design two new droids to act as Darth Vader's caregivers—the ones that, following the Emperor's dictates, turn his burned demi-corpse into a mechanical man.

▲ THE EMPEROROR'S SHUTTLE
Church

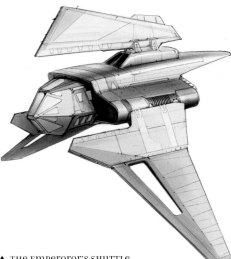

▲ NABOO SHUTTLE, REVISION
Church

▲ SUPER BATTLE DROIDS CLOSING
GENERATOR ROOM DOORS
Tiemens

▲ GENERATOR ROOM/FUEL, LIGHTING
Tiemens

▼ RADIAL MEDICAL DROID, REVISED
Church

"The Polis Massans were designed as very benign. Since we'd be cross-cutting, I wanted these to look like a kid's worst nightmare."—CHURCH

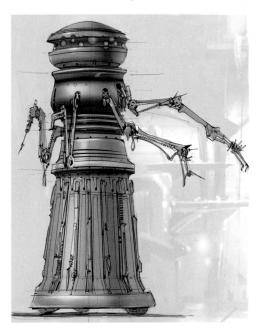

"One of my favorite [industrial designs] of the original series was the AT-ST, the chicken walker. So I decided to design the precursor."—FRAME

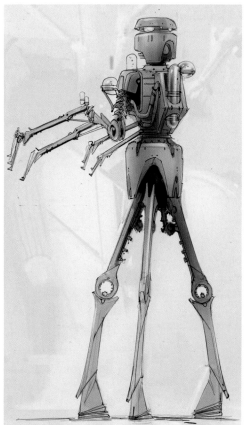

▲ TRI-PEDAL MEDICAL DROID, REVISED
Church

▼ PROTO CHICKEN-WALKER (AT-RT)
Frame

▲ grievous's secret hangar
Church

▲ lizard wrangler eye, closing
Jun

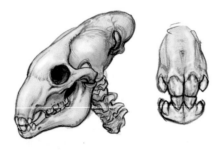

"We've started set construction; costumes have been pumping up . . . Everything is moving. We're heading for a destination, but we're not sure where we're gonna end up."—McCallum

◄ lizard wrangler skull & jaw
Jun

▲ conference room
Zhu

▲ UTAPAU PLANTS
Thompson

utapau esoterica

MAY 16–JUNE 3, 2003

As the preproduction phase nears its end, the artists concentrate on details such as plants and characters' eyes. Lucas approves these, and also signs off on Grievous's secret hangar.

▲ LIZARD SADDLE, TOP VIEW
Jun-McCaig

▼▶ BOGA GESTURES
Jun

▲ DEATH STAR CONSTRUCTION
Church

"The question was: Where are they building the
Death Star? George didn't buy the building ships,
for scale reasons, so that will be revised." —CHURCH

▼ SENATE SECRET CHAMBER, POD LOWERED
Church

THE LAST DIGITAL PICTURE SHOW

JUNE 13, 2003

After a year of intense conceptual brainstorming
and the creation of nearly three thousand artworks, the big conceptual push is over. By the
end of the month, the department—which
McCallum often likened to a jazz ensemble—will
have been broken up. Some will return to ILM,
others will go to work on other shows, while only
Tiemens and Church will stay behind to fulfill
the more limited needs of production during
principal photography.

"We got an emergency phone call from George in Sydney, and he described this new room where Yoda and Palpatine face off for the first time. He described it exactly: a couch in one corner; desks in another; a hologram in another. He described how this whole thing retracts and Palpatine just steps off."—CHURCH

▲ SECRET CHAMBER
Tiemens

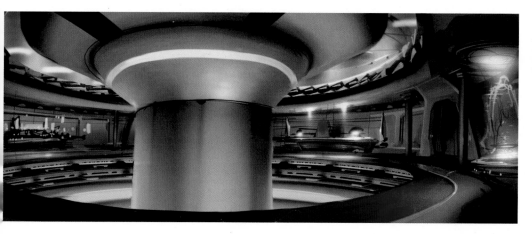

◄ SENATE SECRET CHAMBER, POD RAISED
Church

"Have fun, guys. I'll come back with a movie... The best is yet to come."—LUCAS, *DURING THE LAST ART DEPARTMENT MEETING BEFORE LEAVING FOR SYDNEY, AUSTRALIA*

PART II—PRINCIPAL PHOTOGRAPHY

At Twentieth Century Fox Studios in Sydney, Australia, principal photography for *Revenge of the Sith* begins on June 30, 2003, and finishes on September 17, after fifty-eight days of shooting. During this time, although the Skywalker Ranch concept art department continues to function in a limited capacity, production's output is multiplied exponentially, requiring the efforts

of hundreds of craftspeople, costume creators, and technicians, along with the participation of more than a dozen departments—the largest being the Australia art department, which oversees set design and construction. All of these interrelated groups, covering the full spectrum of disciplines, actually began their preparations months before—but as of Shoot Day 1, everything takes on a much more urgent life. . . .

Note: *The dates given signify the day or days when each set or costume saw its brief but exciting time before the cameras—though it all actually took weeks or months to prepare. Sets are the combined efforts of the Australia art department team, under the direction of production designer Gavin Bocquet. All costumes are the combined work of the costume department under the direction of Trisha Biggar. Likewise, the creatures were made under the supervision of Dave Elsey.*

▲ CONTROL PANEL (Stevens); PADMÉ'S GREEN-CUT VELVET COSTUME (DETAIL); GRIEVOUS'S STARFIGHTER COCKPIT (INTERIOR DETAIL); TRADE FEDERATION CRUISER VENT SHAFT (DETAIL)

▶ QUEEN OF NABOO, HEADDRESS & COSTUME (KEISHA CASTLE-HUGHES)

144

TRADE FEDERATION CRUISER INTERIORS

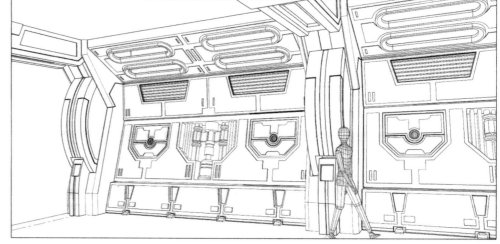

JUNE 30–JULY 1, 2003

Production designer Gavin Bocquet and supervising art director Peter Russell had opened a small-scale Episode III art department at Elstree Studios, London, back in October 2002. Staying in constant communication with Lucas and producer Rick McCallum, they worked there until January 2003, after which production took up residence in Sydney. As head of the art department, Bocquet oversees not only the draftspeople, art directors, and assistant art directors, but also the construction, set decoration, props, and scenic painting departments. Whether massive or seemingly insignificant, every item that goes before the camera receives an astonishing amount of care and effort: the cruiser interiors, though shot on for only two days, took approximately six weeks to build.

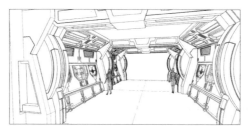

▲ **FEDERATION CRUISER INTERIOR HALLWAY PERSPECTIVES**
Leong

"Two days before shooting on the cruiser interiors—which were going to be very clean and crisp, looking like the Death Star—George decided to make them very grungy, with a worn, battle-scarred look."—GAVIN BOCQUET

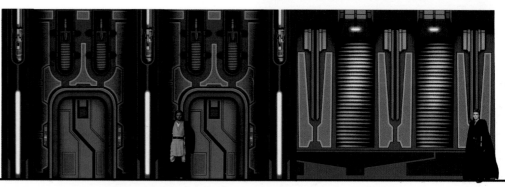

▼▶ CRUISER HALLWAY DETAILS & VENT SHAFT LIGHTS, SETS   ▲ FEDERATION CRUISER HALLWAY AND ELEVATOR LOBBY ELEVATIONS AND COLORS

146

▲▶ PADMÉ (PORTMAN) IN THE AQUA GEORGETTE COSTUME (SCENE 116, JULY 7)

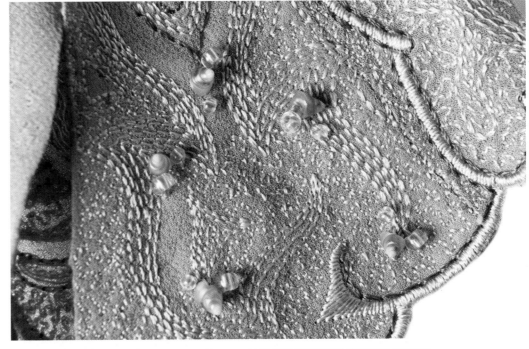

▲▼ AQUA GEORGETTE COSTUME, DETAILS

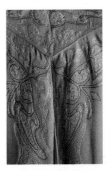

"Padmé ended up with 12 costumes this time, having in Episode II 18, and in Episode I probably 10 or 11. We initially thought she would have fewer costumes this time but, as always, it worked out there were more."—COSTUME DESIGNER *TRISHA BIGGAR*

▲ PEACOCK & BROWN DRESS, DETAIL

◀▲ PADMÉ (PORTMAN) IN THE PEACOCK & BROWN DRESS & DETAIL (SCENE 89, JULY 15)

▶ CONTROL PANEL DETAIL IN ANTECHAMBER

Corridor   Ante Room

▲ PALPATINE'S OFFICE SET FLOOR-PLAN

PALPATINE'S OFFICE COMPLEX

▲ CONCEPTS FOR CORRIDOR STATUE
Stevens

JULY 15–18, 2003

"We're happy that George approves something in a loose way [at the concept art stage], because we're designers and we like to have more room." Bocquet says. "On a normal film, we wouldn't be getting most of this concept art. We'd be developing it all ourselves—but there's so much work on this, I'm not going to say we don't need it! [laughs] We would've been here for two years trying to get that together."

"First, we made some very simple physical models. So I gave Nick [Tory] and Chris [Penn, art department assistants] the plans and drawings we'd done and I gave them the colors to put on. Then we started adding little details, like the chairs that Richard [Roberts, set decorator] had designed; Gert [Stevens, concept artist] did two new statues."—BOCQUET

▲ CONTROL PANELS IN ANTECHAMBER, SET

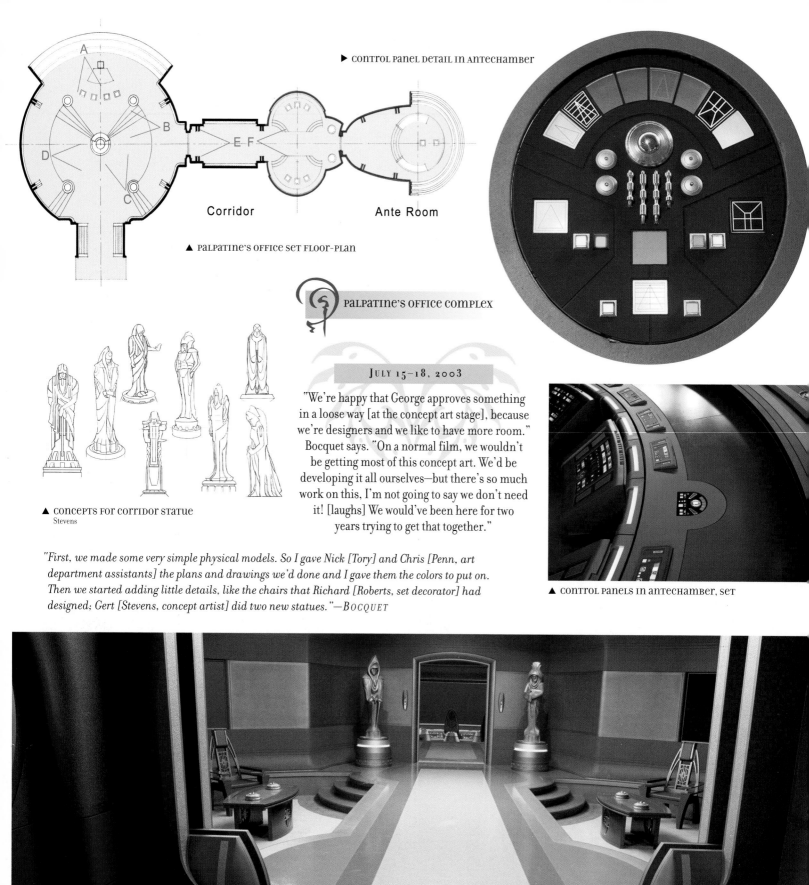

▲ HALLWAY AND WAITING ROOM TO PALPATINE'S ANTECHAMBER, SET

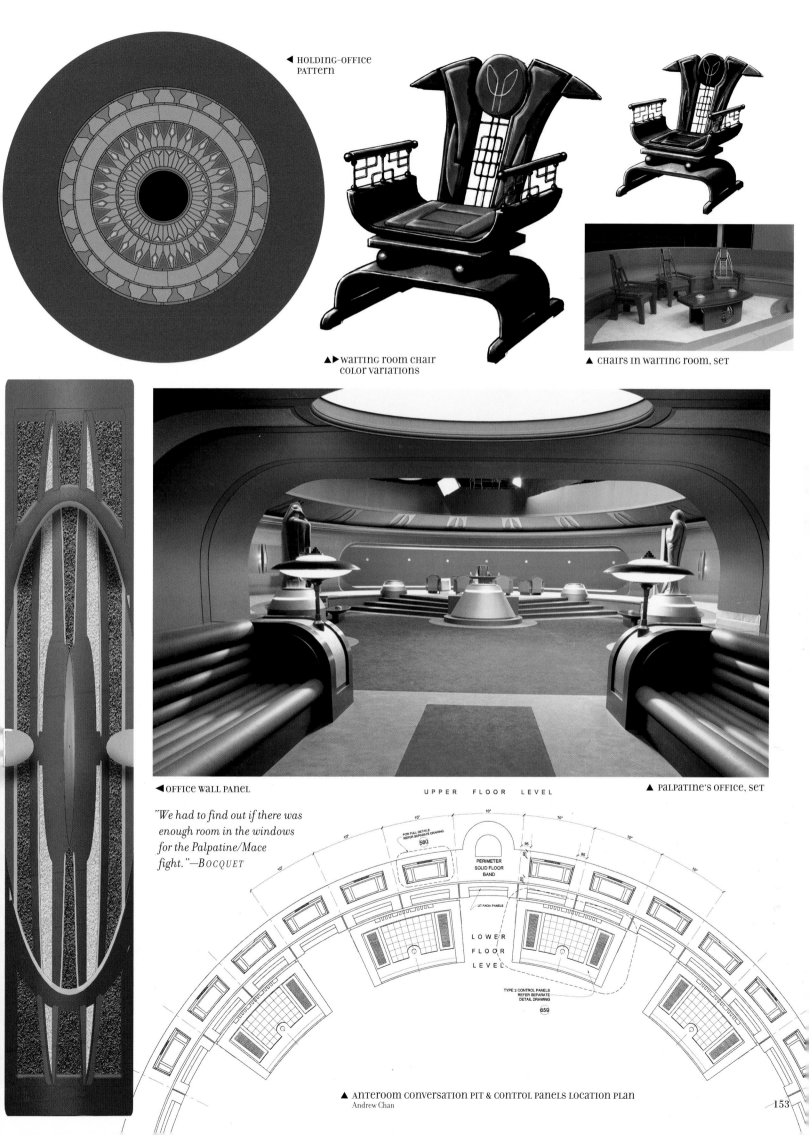

◀ HOLDING-OFFICE
PATTERN

▲▶ WAITING ROOM CHAIR
COLOR VARIATIONS

▲ CHAIRS IN WAITING ROOM, SET

◀ OFFICE WALL PANEL

UPPER   FLOOR   LEVEL

▲ PALPATINE'S OFFICE, SET

"We had to find out if there was
enough room in the windows
for the Palpatine/Mace
fight."—BOCQUET

LOWER
FLOOR
LEVEL

▲ ANTEROOM CONVERSATION PIT & CONTROL PANELS LOCATION PLAN
Andrew Chan

153

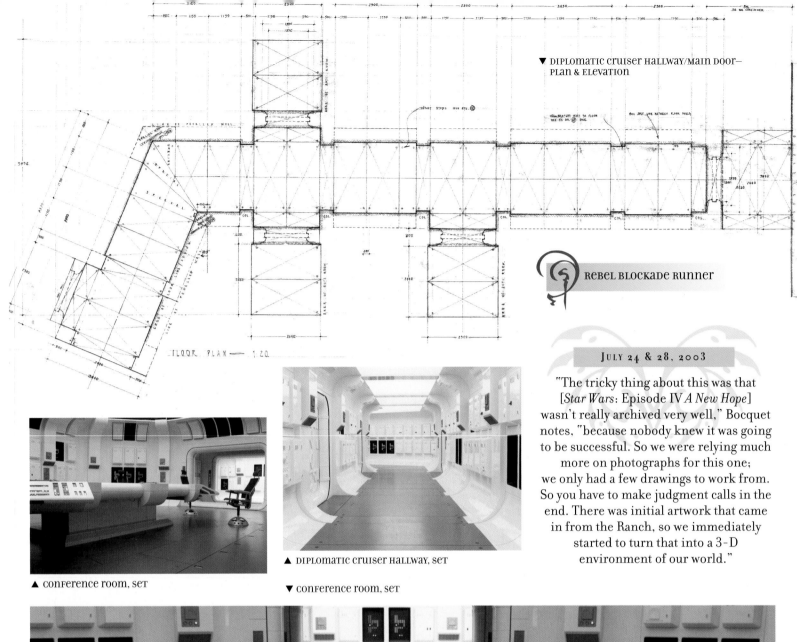

▼ DIPLOMATIC CRUISER HALLWAY/MAIN DOOR–
PLAN & ELEVATION

FLOOR PLAN — 1:20

REBEL BLOCKADE RUNNER

JULY 24 & 28, 2003

"The tricky thing about this was that
[*Star Wars*: Episode IV *A New Hope*]
wasn't really archived very well," Bocquet
notes, "because nobody knew it was going
to be successful. So we were relying much
more on photographs for this one;
we only had a few drawings to work from.
So you have to make judgment calls in the
end. There was initial artwork that came
in from the Ranch, so we immediately
started to turn that into a 3-D
environment of our world."

▲ DIPLOMATIC CRUISER HALLWAY, SET

▲ CONFERENCE ROOM, SET

▼ CONFERENCE ROOM, SET

▲ VIEW OF STOOLS & HALLWAY, SET

▲ MEDICAL DROID
Jaeger

POLIS MASSA MEDICAL CENTER

JULY 25, 2003

"On the Polis Massa viewing station, George really felt that we needed four chairs outside the viewing windows, just stools," Bocquet remarks. "But we only had six hours to make them, so Ty [Teiger, property master] and Richard [Roberts] ran off to the prop room and went through all their junkyard pieces and came up with four really great stools, made up of bits of old pipe-work."

▲ WALL DETAIL, SET

▲ REVISED MEDICAL DROID
Tiemens

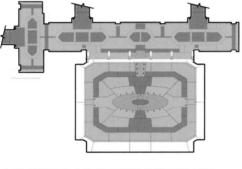

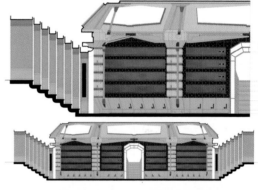

▲ SETOUT PLAN, LONGITUDINAL SECTIONAL PLAN
Anderson

▼ VIEW OF OPERATING ROOM & TABLE, SET

155

SENATE GARB & PROSTHETICS

JULY–SEPTEMBER, 2003

Ian McDiarmid, in his Darth Sidious makeup, wears red robes for his speech in the Senate during which he informs the assembly that he has crushed the Jedi rebellion and inaugurated the Empire. The creatures department, which created the Sidious makeup, is housed at the far eastern end of the studio. It employs a foam lab supervisor, fabrication supervisor, chief animatronic engineer, chief mould maker, prosthetic makeup artists, hair technicians, a sculptor, and a runner—and is all supervised by Dave Elsey, while its smooth running is the responsibility of Rebecca Hunt. With regards to the Neimoidians, Elsey says: "The original Neimoidians, I believe, were made in great haste, as they were originally going to be CG characters, and their lip synching capabilities were basic. We rebuilt these from the ground up, using the original sculpts as a starting point.

The first thing we noticed was that they all wore big hats, so we asked Trisha if this would also be the case for Episode III. When she said it would, the question of where to put the servos was answered. We also worked very closely with Gilderfluke [a robotic and sound systems company] to create a custom-designed computer control system. This ensured that lip synching was perfect, whilst allowing our puppeteers the freedom of improvising on set."

▶ NEIMOIDIAN NUTE GUNRAY (SILAS CARSON, SCENE 52, 130, 135, 142, AUGUST 25 AND SEPTEMBER 8 & 16)

▲ EMPEROR PALPATINE

▲ ALIEN SENATOR (LUKE HINKSMAN, SCENE 175, SEPTEMBER 16)

▲ PO NUDO (PAUL NICHOLSON, SCENE 52, 130 & 135, AUGUST 25 AND SEPTEMBER 8 & 16)

"I love the Emperor. Re-creating that makeup was both a challenge and an honor. I discovered when I rewatched the movie that you could hardly see it. My imagination then took over with all the strange things I thought might be under the hood. Of course, when we talked to George, he knew exactly what was under the hood and was able to rein us in."—DAVE ELSEY

▲▶ PADMÉ (PORTMAN) IN THE PURPLE SENATE GOWN (SCENE 137, JULY 29)

▲ PALPATINE (IAN MCDIARMID) IN THE RED SENATE COSTUME (SCENE 137, JULY 29)

▲ BD3000 DROID, REVISED HAIR
Tiemens

► BD3000 DROID
Jaeger

▼ FEMALE ROBOT STUDY
Tiemens

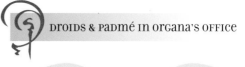

JULY 30, 2003

Scaled down to only a few artists, the concept art department back at Skywalker Ranch receives a call one day from animation director Rob Coleman, who is on the set in Sydney. Lucas has requested that a female robot servant be added to a scene in Bail Organa's office. The day of the shoot, a woman clad in a blue suit acts as a placeholder (the droid, of course, will be added much later in postproduction).

▲▼ ORGANA'S OFFICE CARPET & WALL DETAILS

"We're not really like other designers, because most others—fashion designers, architectural design-ers—they're all in a sense fashion oriented. They're all about new standards of design, whereas our design is purely based on the script."—BOCQUET

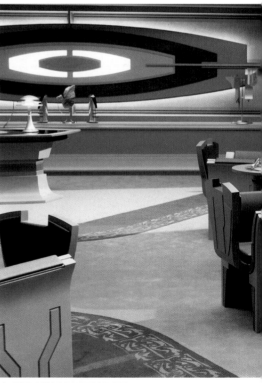

▲ BAIL ORGANA'S OFFICE, SET

158

"We see Padmé in Bail Organa's office. There's a formal quality required there, and the people she's meeting with are not to be aware that she's pregnant. So for that costume I wanted to have a feel of the ceremonial."—BIGGAR

▼▶ PADMÉ (PORTMAN) IN THE BURGUNDY VELVET COSTUME (SCENE 60, JULY 30)

"On Episode II, while we were here in Australia, I discovered a marvelous embroiderer—Sandra Faltin. So we've been doing lots of embroidery, different types, different techniques."—BIGGAR

▲ BURGUNDY VELVET COSTUME, DETAIL

TRADE FEDERATION CRUISER BRIDGE

AUGUST 1 & 4, 2003

According to head scenic artist Matt Connors, "The hardest bit is doing the colors. The set is first painted with basic house paints. The team then ages the paint with wax, putting in scuffs and handprints around the doors." *Revenge of the Sith* reveals a time when the trappings of the Republic are beginning to crumble under the onslaught of the Clone Wars, so, as Connors points, out, "there's a lot more aging in this one; it's a bit bolder."

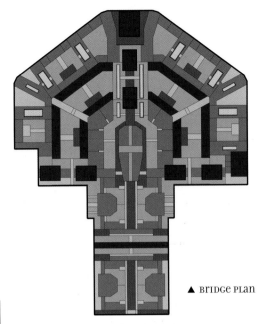

▲ BRIDGE PLAN

▲ NAVIGATOR'S CHAIR CONCEPTS
Stevens

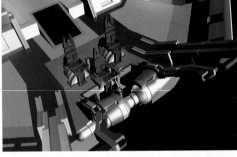

▲ NAVIGATOR'S CHAIR, 3-D RENDER

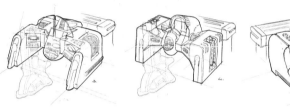

▲ CONSOLE CONCEPTS
Stevens

▲ BRIDGE, NAVIGATOR'S CHAIR, SET

▲ VIEW OF OBI-WAN'S GREEN JEDI STARFIGHTER COCKPIT, SET

▲ COCKPIT INTERIOR, SET

▼ JEDI STARFIGHTER DETAILS, SET

▲ STARFIGHTER CANNON, SET

▲ STARFIGHTER CONTROL PANEL READOUT DETAILS

▼ GRIEVOUS'S STARFIGHTER, COLOR, SIDE-VIEW
Church

▲ GRIEVOUS'S STARFIGHTER STEERING CONTROLS, SET

▲ GRIEVOUS'S STARFIGHTER DETAILS, SET

SEPTEMBER 3–4, 2003

"The general thing we were trying to do," says Bocquet, "is connect Episode III's design with the original trilogy. Somebody said, 'These sets look like *Star Wars* sets.' And that's because we have arrived at a language in the third film where there is a seamless fit into that world."

"Any designer worth his or her salt designs to help the camera operator. Gavin [Bocquet] would build in lots of practical places to put the lights."—RUSSELL

◀ GENERAL'S QUARTERS COLUMN DETAIL, SET

▼ DOORWAY ELEVATION

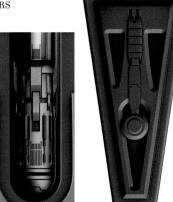

▲ WALL DETAIL CONCEPTS

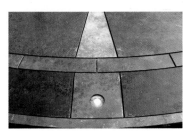

▲ FLOOR DETAIL, SET

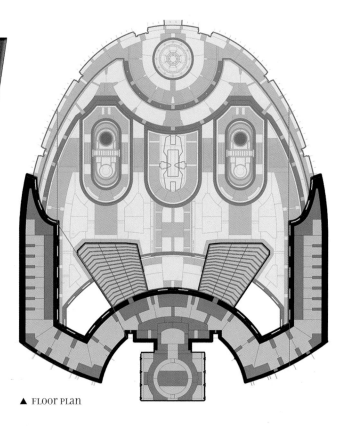

▲ FLOOR PLAN

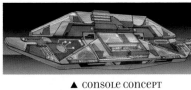

▲ CONSOLE CONCEPT

"No one person on the film can let anyone else down, because it has a ripple effect on the whole picture. It's incredibly collaborative—most people don't realize how collaborative it is, how intensely personal, how emotionally draining."
—MCCALLUM

◀ FLOOR LAMP CONCEPTS (INSETS)
Stevens

▲ VIEW FROM BALCONY TO CHAIR, SET

PART III—DIGITAL SHOT CREATION

After principal photography wraps, the Skywalker Ranch art department's mission statement changes. Though relatively dormant during the three-month production period, with only the occasional call for an opera box or a droid design, it now expands, as many other departments suddenly need their services: animatics, computer and practical model-makers, view-paint, digi-matte painting, and so on.

Tiemens and Church therefore divide their time between Skywalker Ranch—where they still create conceptual designs while interfacing with the animatics group—and ILM, where Tiemens works with the digi-matte artists, and Church with the CG vehicle modelers. Also at ILM, Aaron McBride aids CG creature makers, while Alex Jaeger concentrates on CG vehicles and hardware.

Meanwhile, shot by shot, Lucas slowly begins to cut together *Revenge of the Sith*—with editorial ultimately driving the need for new artwork. . . .

Note: *Three-letter acronyms are used to designate scene locales; subsequent single digits indicate whether it's the first, second, or third scene to take place in that locale. The following numbers refer to the shot.*

▲ CRYSTAL WORLD, DIGI-MATTE CONCEPT (Church); DAGOBAH SWAMP CONCEPT 01 (Tiemens)

▶ CPA (CORUSCANT PADMÉ'S APARTMENT)—VIEW OF DINING HALL FROM VERANDA MATTE PAINTING CONCEPT 02
Tiemens

▲ CORUSCANT DIGI-MATTE CONCEPT
Dusseault

"We had to show what was outside Palpatine's new antechamber. The script says it's twilight. The digi-matte painting department will eventually make it photo-real. They use their library of buildings to match the shapes; if there's new stuff, they custom-build it." —CHURCH

▶ PALPATINE'S OFFICE, TWILIGHT CYCLORAMA
Church

"You don't get the camera way back very often during a film. Everything else is just talking heads against backgrounds. So every wide shot is a signature shot." —LUCAS

GOLDEN AND DARK CORUSCANT

AUGUST–DECEMBER 2003

While Fay David is visiting the set in early August, producer Rick McCallum asks, "Can I talk to you about matte paintings?" Their conversation leads to a conversation with Lucas, which leads to certain Coruscant locations being designated as future digi-matte painting environments: Padmé's veranda (CPV), day and evening; the Chancellor's office, twilight (CCM) and day (CCO); and the Jedi Temple (CJC), day and evening. As soon as she returns to California, David meets with Church, Tiemens, digi-matte painting supervisor Jonathan Harb, and digi-matte artist Yanick Dusseault. Harb actually attended concept art department meetings as early as January 2003. After flying from New Zealand where he'd just finished working on *The Lord of the Rings*, Dusseault was introduced to Lucas in March. Following the August meeting, the ILM Episode III digi-matte painting department is kicked into gear.

▼ CSL: CORUSCANT SENATE LANDING PLATFORM
Church

▶ CBO: CORUSCANT BAIL ORGANA'S OFFICE
Tiemens

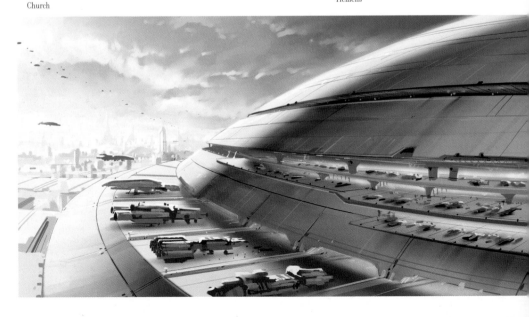

172

▲ Naboo skiff landing platform, digi-matte concept
Dusseault

▼ SC. 66 CPV: Coruscant Padmé veranda, digi-matte concept
Dusseault

▶ SC. 66 CPV: Coruscant Padmé veranda,
digi-matte concept
Dusseault

"A film used to have maybe 10 to 50 effects shots;
we have at least 2000. Where you once had a million
dollars in effects shots, now you have 40 or 50
million dollars worth. On Revenge, the production
crew worked for 9 months, the shooting crew for
3 months—but the visual effects crew will work for
18 months. And even as big as our sets were, we
only spent about 4.5 million dollars on all of them
combined. We'll spend 10 million dollars on our
digital sets."—McCallum

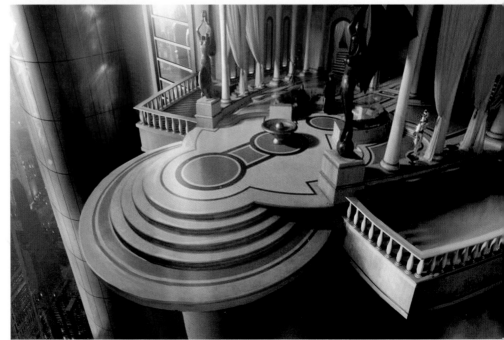

▲ CSL: coruscant senate landing platform, digi-matte concept
Dusseault

▼ CJR.015: coruscant jedi return—digi-matte concept
Dusseault

"I did a solid six months of concept matte paintings—one a day—to bridge the art department to the digi-matte department. I'd talk with Erik and Ryan, and they would show me what they'd done so far. Then I'd take their artwork and build on it to define the actual shots for the movie, coming up with sharp images, locked off and more defined in terms of composition and color palette."—YANICK DUSSEAULT

▲ CJG: jedi embarkation center, cloud colors
Tiemens

▲ CJG. 200: coruscant jedi gunship
Church

▲ CTC: CORUSCANT JEDI TEMPLE CONTROL ROOM,
UNDAMAGED/DAMAGED
McBride

▼ JEDI TEMPLE GROUND-LEVEL INTERIOR, ENTRANCE DETAIL
McBride

▲ JEDI TEMPLE ENTRANCE
McBride

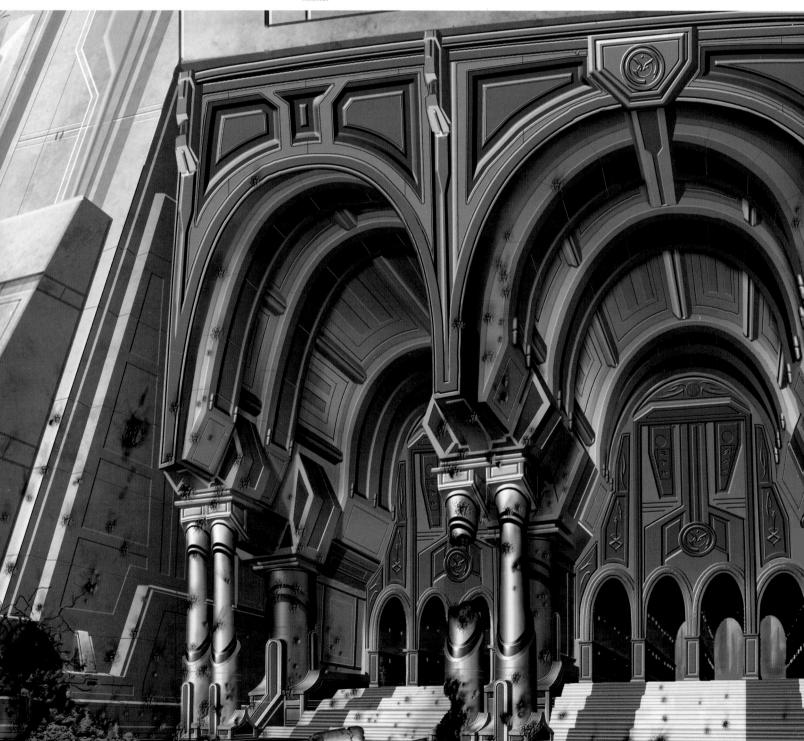

▲ JEDI TEMPLE SKY VIEW
Tiemens

► TEMPLE STATUES
McBride

OCTOBER–DECEMBER 2003

In-between morning and late-afternoon editing sessions, Lucas passes two to three hours nearly everyday, from October 2003 to September 2004, in the animatics department. Here, with the aid of a dozen or so animartists—led by previsualization supervisor Dan Gregoire—he directs many scenes that will be all or primarily computer-generated, slowly creating low-resolution three-dimensional sequences. After Lucas creates a satisfactory edit of each scene, he turns it over to ILM, where it is made photo-real. As he builds these sequences and decides where the camera should go, art requirements become evident. Church and Tiemens therefore take a seat behind Lucas as he directs. "George was coming up with shots on the fly," Church says.

► TEMPLE STATUE MODEL
Miller & ILM model shop

"I was looking over George's shoulder as he was directing Eric Carney. They were working on the animatics of the scene where Yoda and Obi-Wan sneak into the Jedi Temple, and George wanted to boom [crane] down to the entrance—but there was nothing there—because nothing had been designed yet. So I ran back to my desk and drew up this idea during the meeting, and they slapped it into the animatics. Later Aaron [McBride] refined it to take it to the next level."
—CHURCH

▲ JEDI TEMPLE FAÇADE BAS RELIEF
Church

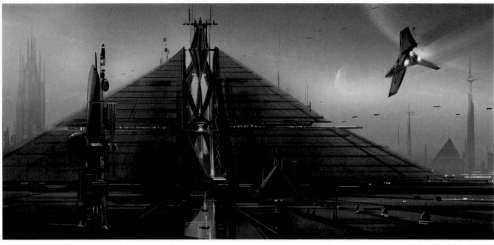

▲ CRL: CORUSCANT REHABILITATION LANDING PLATFORM, THUMBNAIL CONCEPT 01
Tiemens

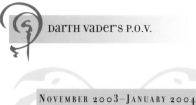

NOVEMBER 2003–JANUARY 2004

Although the interior of the rehabilitation center—where Darth Vader is transformed from man to machine—was designed prior to principal photography, its exterior is tackled in post.

"I looked at some early Ralph McQuarrie concept paintings, and he'd done some interesting pyramid structures."—TIEMENS

▲ CRL: CORUSCANT REHABILITATION LANDING PLATFORM, THUMBNAIL CONCEPT 02
Tiemens

▲ REHAB CENTER, DARTH VADER'S POINT-OF-VIEW—LOOKING OUT
Dusseault

178

"I wanted to hint that the mask is painful to wear, with lots of pointy things that poke Vader as it interfaces with him."
—CHURCH

179

DECEMBER 2003–JANUARY 2004

While working with the animatics group and in editorial, Lucas necessarily swaps objects, vehicles, and locations. A clone commander may begin on Utapau but end up on Kashyyyk. Likewise, a dragonfly might begin as Yoda's steed on Kashyyyk, and end up ridden by another alien species on Utapau.

▲ WIND PLANET, OR DUSTWORLD—EARLY SALEUCAMI
Church

▶ CAPITAL SHIP OVER MYGEETO
Church

"I'd designed the spider-like creature way back and I just kept putting it in environments. I also kept trying to get this image of the Republic assault ship into the film. Though this painting is on Mygeeto [right], the shot eventually wound up as part of the Utapau sequence."—CHURCH

▶ SALEUCAMI BATTLE
Tiemens

▼ MYGEETO, ATTACK OF THE SPIDER DROIDS
Church

▲ DAGOBAH POD LANDING CONFIGURATION
Jaeger

"A problem arose with the pod design, which was requiring Yoda to walk down a long ramp. I saw the fins as the solution to the problem, and came up with the idea that they would fold outward to create a shorter ramp and a more elegant landing."—JAEGER

JANUARY 2004

Although this scene is ultimately cut from the film, many concept paintings are created showing Yoda's arrival on Dagobah, the planet first seen in 1980s *The Empire Strikes Back*. The Jedi Master was to have been seen going into exile after the fall of the Jedi, but Lucas decides that the film—with brief finales on Naboo, aboard a Star Destroyer, and on Tatooine—has too many endings.

▲ YODA LANDS, DOWN SHOT WITH LIGHT
Tiemens

▶ DAGOBAH SWAMP
Tiemens

▲ DAGOBAH ESTABLISHING SHOT 03
Church

▲ MUSTAFAR CYCLORAMA LAVASCAPE VERSION 03
Tiemens

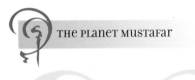

THE PLANET MUSTAFAR

DECEMBER 2003–FEBRUARY 2004

Building on what had been established during preproduction, and what was shot in Sydney, production's attention turns toward Mustafar. At first the artists work in general strokes, but soon much more definition will be needed . . .

▶ MUSTAFAR
Church

"This was the first concept of Mustafar seen from space."—CHURCH

"I love this new digital world. We can just keep adding to it until it's right in the end."—LUCAS

▼ LAVA CYCLORAMA
Tiemens

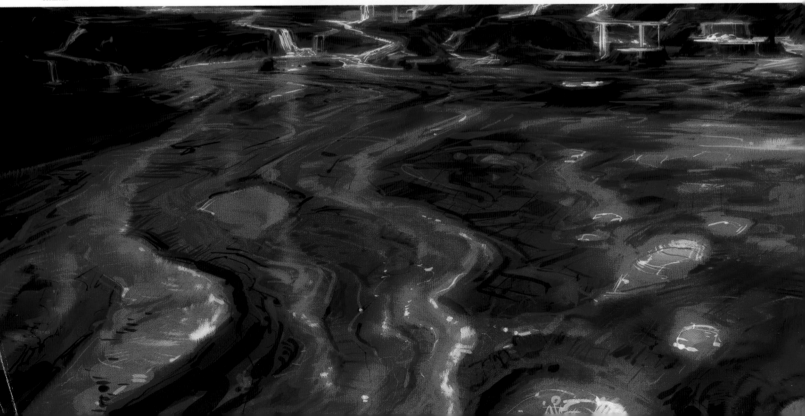

"Before we even got into the animatics, George needed fillers so he could see what Anakin was contemplating as he thought about what he just did."—TIEMENS

▼ LAVA version 02
Tiemens

▲ YODA FOUND BY CLONE TROOPERS ON KASHYYYK
Church

"Yoda is doing his first shtick, which we see later in Empire. He's covered in mud, but he's using the Force. In the background, there's wreckage of the burning Wookiee tree. You've got the red lights, which means the clone troopers are now bad guys."—CHURCH

▲ KVL: KASHYYYK VILLAGE LAKE—YODA MUD MASK, VERSION 02
McBride

▲ NIGHT HUNT (PAINTING OVER ANIMATIC)
Church

CLIMATE CHANGES ON KASHYYYK

NOVEMBER 2003–FEBRUARY 2004

Among the first edited sequences Lucas turns over to ILM are those featuring Yoda. Most of them are fairly straightforward scenes with the Jedi Master either sitting or walking. One scene looming on the horizon, however, will have Yoda feigning madness—a complex moment that requires early work on Yoda's look.

"We went through a transition from a tropical Kashyyyk, with clear water, to George wanting a kind of clear haze where the mountains step back [right]."—TIEMENS

186

◄ color temperatures of kashyyyk establishing shot
Church

▲ kashyyyk mist
Tiemens

◄ color temperatures of kashyyyk establishing shot, revised
Church

◀ coruscant galactic opera, exterior
Church

▲ opera staircase
Church

▲ opera house box, practical model
ILM model shop

◀ opera entrance
Church

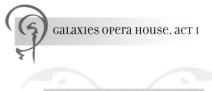

GALAXIES OPERA HOUSE, ACT I

JUNE 2003–MARCH 2004

Back in July, following a Saturday run-through at Fox Studios, Australia, Lucas changes the locale of the scene in which Palpatine tells Anakin about the dark side. "During rehearsal, I said, 'My God, this is a four-page scene—I've had five scenes in the Chancellor's office already—how am I going to do this?' So I put it in an opera house, watching a ballet—*Squid Lake*—which worked out great." The call goes out to Fay, who calls Church requesting four illustrations. All that's required at that time is the box and the seats; now in post, what Anakin and Palpatine are looking at from the box, and the opera house itself, needs to be conceptualized.

"We got approval on the antigravity water ball that the Mon Calamari swim through, so I knew the exterior of the building could be spherical. Originally, I had the environment more cropped in, but George kept saying he wanted to see more, so I kept zooming out."—CHURCH

▲ OPERA BOX CONCEPT
Church

"I drive home at the end of a hard day, and George drives home. And he comes back to work and I come back—but the stuff that happens to him from the time he leaves to the time he comes back is just incredible... Every day, there's a new idea coming in. And it's just a fantastic way to work."—McCALLUM

▼ CGO.030: CORUSCANT GALAXIES OPERA HOUSE CONCEPT
Church

▲ OPERA BOX P.O.V.
Church

189

Because there is a long almost roadlike lead-in to the opera house, Lucas decides that air limousines will pull up to the "curb," where droid valets will greet them. In addition to the "Mon Calamari dancers," as McCallum names them, opera-goers and their costumes have to be designed, which prompts the return of concept artist Sang Jun Lee. In his February 17 critique of Jun's first sketches, Lucas asks for the dresses to be "sexier, formal, more glamorous."

"We'd seen Admiral Ackbar, who's older, so this is a pass at what a younger Mon Calamari dancer might look like—one who'd been working out nearly every waking moment."
—McBride

◄ FEMALE COSTUME 10
Jun

▲ MON CALAMARI FEMALE DANCER
McBride

▲ OPERA LIMOUSINE 02
Church

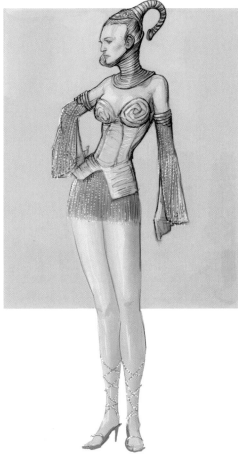

"George wanted to see different cultures in the shot, so I researched formal costumes from different parts of the world: the Middle East, Turkey, Russia, Mongolia."—JUN

▲▼ FEMALE COSTUMES, 07, 12 & 09
Jun

▲ MALE COSTUME 04
Jun

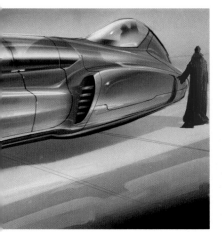

▲ OPERA SPEEDER 01
Church

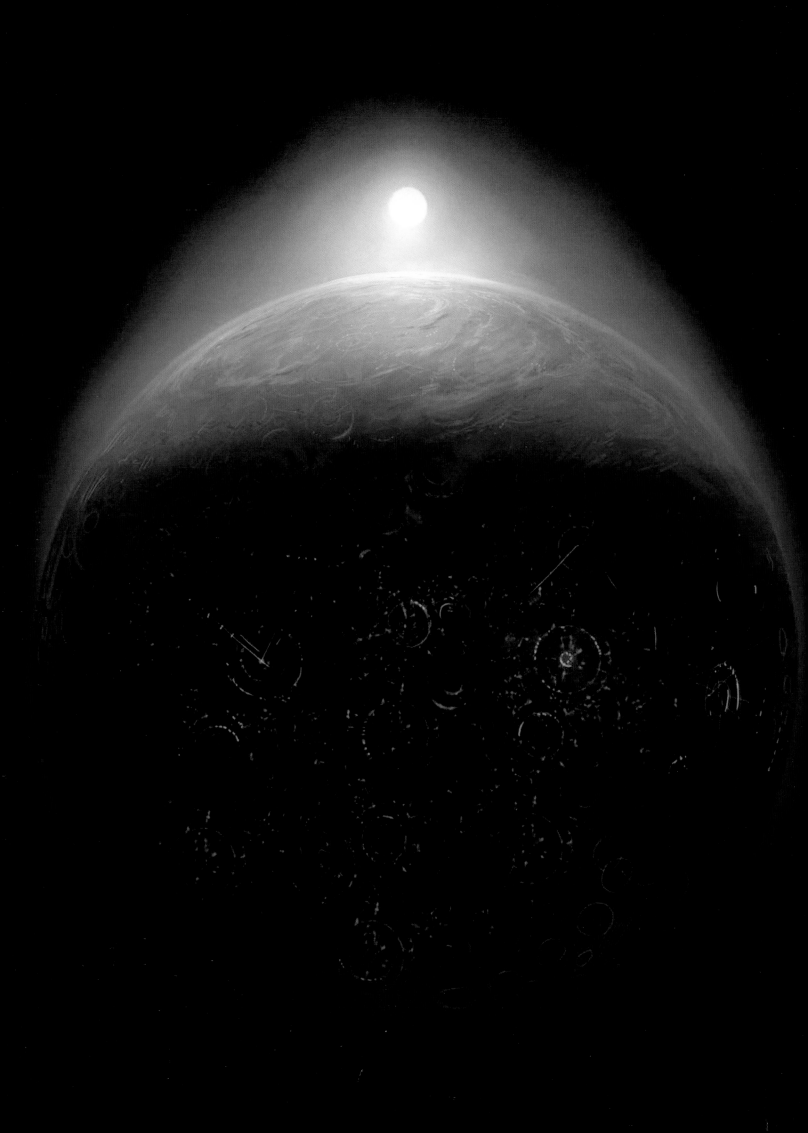

JANUARY–APRIL 2004

On December 8, 2003, Lucas turns over the opening space battle (OSB) to ILM. It consists of more than a hundred shots, but lasts only a few minutes. "Our biggest challenge here is readability," Lucas says. Indeed, the sequence features a potentially confusing array of craft and action. By January 29, ILM's layout department has finished its job of blocking out the action. Meanwhile, concept artists and others work to make the OSB dazzling but audience-friendly. The charge is led by the four concept artists, visual effects supervisor John Knoll, animation supervisor Rob Coleman, 3-D supervisor David Meny, compositing supervisors Eddie Pasquarello and Pat Tubach, 3-D sequence supervisor Neil Herzinger, animation sequence supervisors Scott Benza and Glen McIntosh, modeling supervisor Pam Choy, view paint supervisor Elbert Yen, and lead 3-D artists David Weitzberg, Willi Geiger, and Jean-Paul Beaulieu.

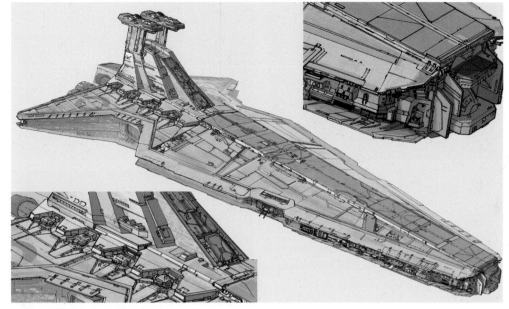

◀ sunrise over coruscant
Tiemens

"This is the lighting scheme we wanted at the very opening of the space battle—an evocative look, with haze and this sunrise, so you can see the curve of the planet and the sun reflected on the spaceships."—TIEMENS

▼ FBG.270: fed cruiser droid guns
Church

▲▶ trade federation cruiser surface details
Don Bies/ILM model shop

▲ jedi cruiser surface detail
Jaeger

"Once we started the opening shots as the starfighters fly over the Jedi cruiser deck, we needed to have an idea of what that looked like up close."—JAEGER

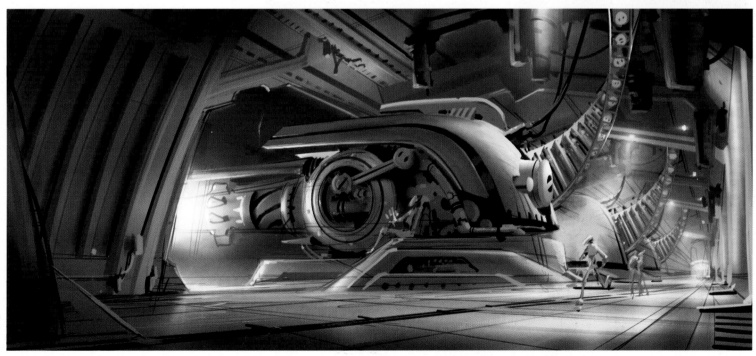

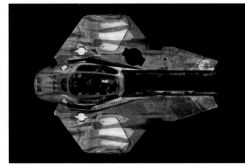
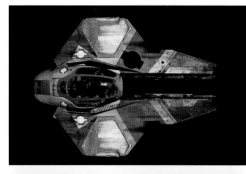

▲▶ JEDI STARFIGHTER HOT-ROD PAINT SCHEMES
Jaeger

▲ SEPARATIST CRUISER SHIELD GENERATOR CONCEPT
Jaeger

"We see the capital ships exchanging massive amounts of fire, so the idea was to design more human-sized guns, as if they were set up inside an old clipper ship."—CHURCH

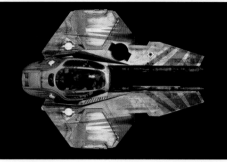

"George asked for something visual on the exterior of the ship that said, If this thing gets damaged, the shield will fail."—JAEGER

▼ CLONE TROOPER SHIP GUNS
Church

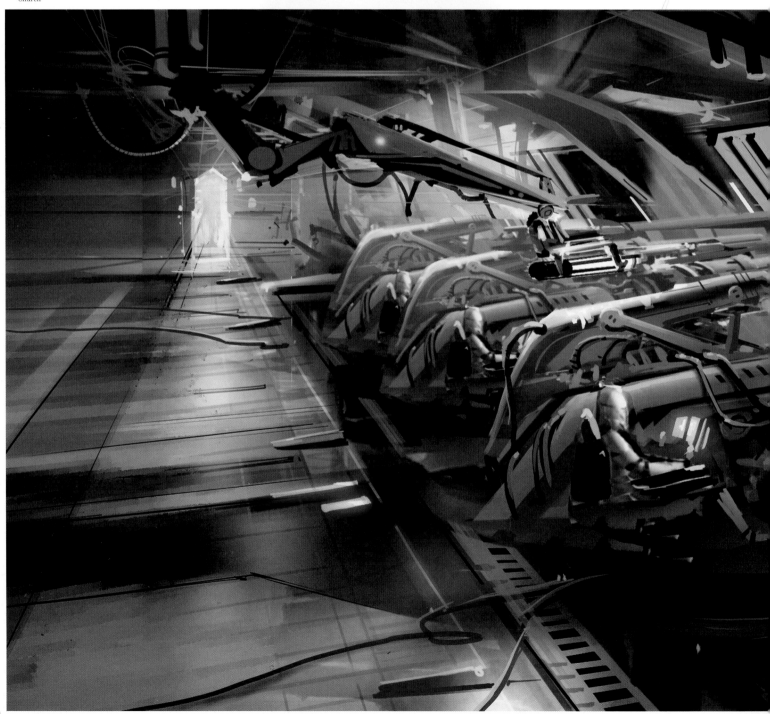

▲ SPACE BATTLE, EXAMPLE FRAME 04
McBride

"This was done on top of an animatics rendering to create scale and lighting, and things like debris trails and giant columns of smoke from wrecked ships being pulled down into the atmosphere."
—AARON MCBRIDE

▶ SPACE BATTLE, EXAMPLE FRAME 01
Jaeger

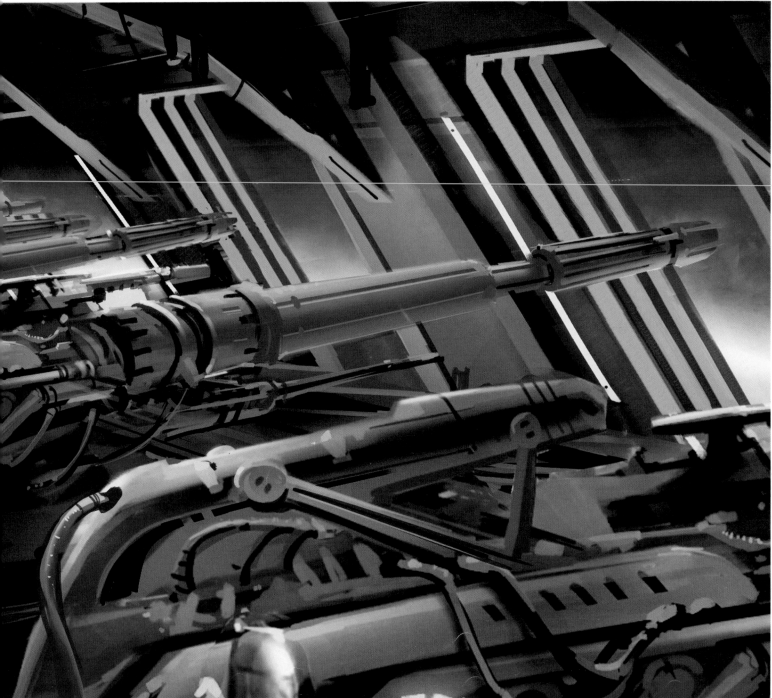

"*This [right] was part of the super detailing process of the clone tank. It was originally part of a sequence in which the turret turned and blasted a Jedi on Kashyyyk.*"
—JAEGER

▶ CLONE TRUCK, REAR TURRET, DETAIL
Jaeger

▲ CLONE HOVER TANK
Jaeger

◀ P.A.W. (POD ATTACK WALKER), REVISED DESIGN
Jaeger

▲ CLONE DROP SHIP (UTAPAU)
Church

► BAIL SPEEDER NEW FRONT DESIGN 03
Jaeger

▼ DC0052 SPEEDER,
COCKPIT DOOR
CONFIGURATION
FOR CG MODELERS
(INSET)
Jaeger

LATER CRAFT

AUGUST 2003–APRIL 2004

As CG scenes are refined, so are the movie's
vehicles. A Republic assault ship becomes
a Separatist assault ship, which becomes
a gunship-sized drop ship for Utapau.
Indeed, as its Clone War escalates, that planet
also receives the newly designed P-38.

▼ UTAPAU FIGHTER CONCEPT (P-38)
Church

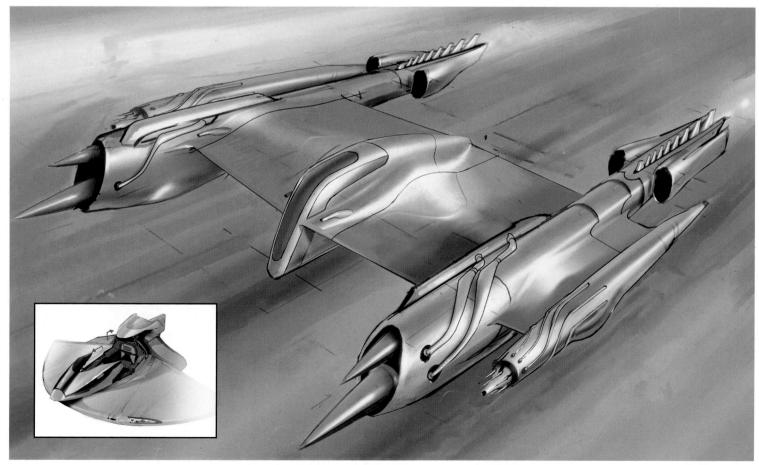

▶ GRIEVOUS BODYGUARDS—A, B, C & D
Jaeger

"These were painted over a gray CG model, as reference for view painters and cloth modelers. 'A' fought something that had sharp talons, and which busted out one of his eyeballs. 'B' did battle with someone equipped with a blaster. 'C' has lots of scorch marks on him, as if he'd fought something that had a flamethrower; 'D' has blood splatters on his cloak." —JAEGER

DRESSED TO THE BLASTER

OCTOBER 2003–MARCH 2004

Lucas's desire for individualized clone trooper armor, as expressed during the very first art department meeting back in April 2002, has a continuing effect throughout postproduction, as Jaeger creates several outfit variations. Though they are essentially dictated by climate, some are takeoffs on the armor seen in the *Clone Wars* cartoons, while others are throwbacks (or throw forwards) to the Episode IV desert stormtroopers.

▼ COMMANDER FAIE [DAVID]
Jaeger

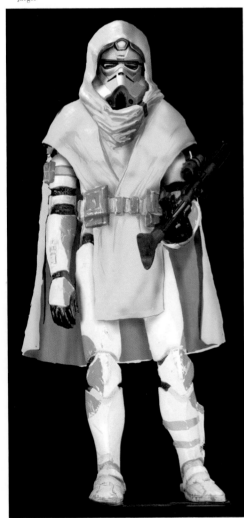

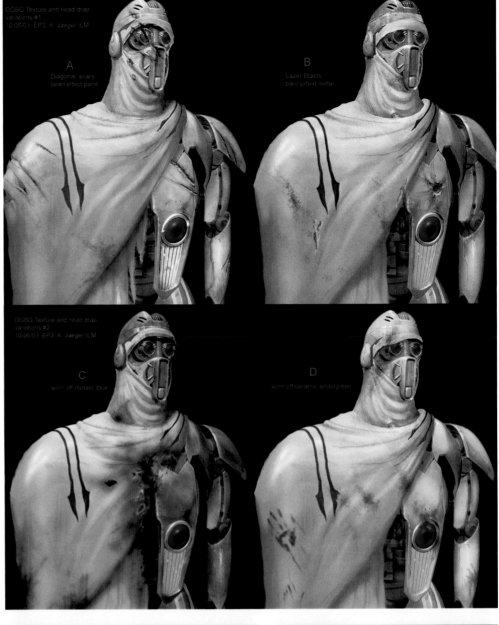

▲ CLONE TANK DRIVER, INCLEMENT-WEATHER HELMET AND SHOULDER PAD
Jaeger

▲ CLONE COMMANDER VARIATIONS D, E, F
Jaeger

▲ ARC TROOPER COLOR VARIATION
Jaeger

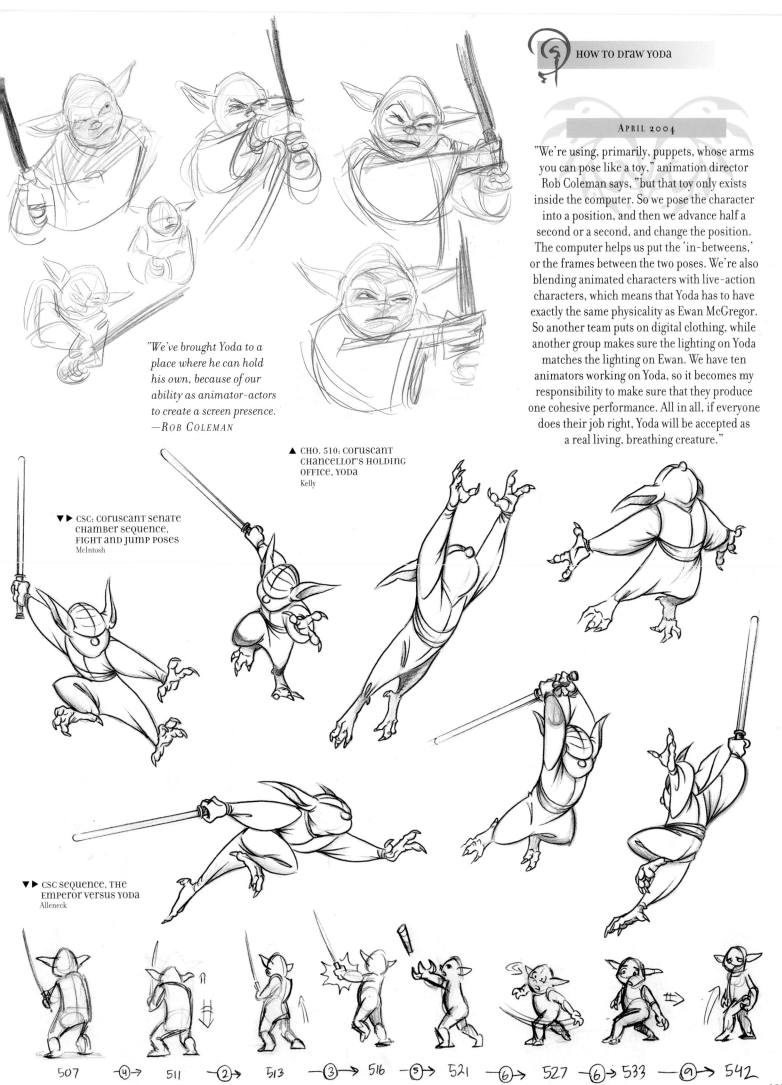

APRIL 2004

"We're using, primarily, puppets, whose arms you can pose like a toy," animation director Rob Coleman says, "but that toy only exists inside the computer. So we pose the character into a position, and then we advance half a second or a second, and change the position. The computer helps us put the 'in-betweens,' or the frames between the two poses. We're also blending animated characters with live-action characters, which means that Yoda has to have exactly the same physicality as Ewan McGregor. So another team puts on digital clothing, while another group makes sure the lighting on Yoda matches the lighting on Ewan. We have ten animators working on Yoda, so it becomes my responsibility to make sure that they produce one cohesive performance. All in all, if everyone does their job right, Yoda will be accepted as a real living, breathing creature."

"We've brought Yoda to a place where he can hold his own, because of our ability as animator-actors to create a screen presence.
—ROB COLEMAN

▲ CHO. 510: CORUSCANT CHANCELLOR'S HOLDING OFFICE, YODA
Kelly

▼▶ CSC: CORUSCANT SENATE CHAMBER SEQUENCE, FIGHT AND JUMP POSES
McIntosh

▼▶ CSC SEQUENCE, THE EMPEROR VERSUS YODA
Alleneck

507 —④→ 511 —②→ 513 —③→ 516 —⑤→ 521 —⑥→ 527 —⑥→ 533 —⑨→ 542

▲ POLIS MASSA CRATER PRACTICAL MODEL
Lorne Peterson & Nelson Hall/ILM model shop

▲ POLIS MASSA HANGAR, DETAILED SET DRESS
Jaeger

"We only see the floor of this now [above right], but we would've seen, laying against the walls, lots of the archaeological findings of the Polis Massans."—JAEGER

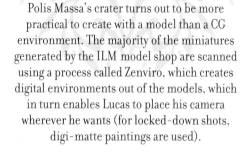
JANUARY–MAY 2004

Polis Massa's crater turns out to be more practical to create with a model than a CG environment. The majority of the miniatures generated by the ILM model shop are scanned using a process called Zenviro, which creates digital environments out of the models, which in turn enables Lucas to place his camera wherever he wants (for locked-down shots, digi-matte paintings are used).

▶ NABOO DAY, DIGI-MATTE CONCEPT
Dusseault-Tiemens

"*The Alderaan cruiser originally arrived at night under moonlight—that's the way Yanick painted it [right]. But then it was revised to dawn, so I repainted it. You can see the rivers in the background, which relate to the funeral the following dawn. George wanted to convey in a predawn setting a somber event, but very populated, as if a beloved queen or king had passed away [below].*"—TIEMENS

▼ NABOO FUNERAL, DIGI-MATTE CONCEPT
Tiemens

NOVEMBER 2003–JULY 2004

While Lucas continues to create rough cuts with his editors Ben Burtt and Roger Barton, the middle sequences of *Revenge of the Sith* undergo many revisions. Scenes are added, deleted, and changed around. As clone troopers carry out Order 66, the number and identities of the Jedi killed vary, as do the planets and their environments. Ring world and Saleucami combine to become Cato Neimoidia, while Felucia's sequences are shortened. Late in the game Saleucami is reborn by taking one of Felucia's discarded environments (Felucia 01, by Jaeger; see page 75) and repurposing it.

▲ SALEUCAMI/CATO NEIMOIDIA
Church

"George had the idea of turning the buildings on Saleucami right-side-up and making that Cato Neimoidia, so it's now hammock world. This is where Plo Koon gets blasted in his starfighter."—CHURCH

▼ CATO NEIMOIDIA INTERIOR
Church

"A long time ago, I'd done the old, gilded world of Cato Neimoidia. I knew George was going to start shooting it, so I wanted to give him the reverse angle. But this is all out of the movie now."—CHURCH

▲ FELUCIA FOREST
Church

"When Josh [Wassung, animatics artist] started working on the Felucia sequence, he wanted to turn his camera around, so he was asking, 'Well, what's over here?' Which prompted more Felucia exploration." —CHURCH

"I was in animatics while George was working on the fly-in to Utapau with Greg [Rizzi]" Church says, "and originally Utapau had these mounds, which were starting to look like Geonosis's towers, and the colors were starting to look like Naboo's and Kashyyyk's. So I did a quick concept of ridge world—whose ridges enhance the feeling of depth, because all these one-point-perspective lines converge. I threw in a huge gas planet, which George went for, and the high mackerel clouds." It was then digi-matte artist Brett Northcutt's turn. "I began by building millions of polygons' worth of terrain in 3ds Max and ended up combining texture photographs of a local ranch, southwestern deserts, and even of the gravel parking lot. Once the painting was complete and projected onto the 3-D geometry, I rendered this shot from a virtual camera slowly flying closer to the surface."

▲ LIZARD'S MATING CALL
McIntosh

▼ UTAPAU WITH PLANETS (INSET)
Church

▼ UTAPAU DIGI-MATTE PAINTING
Northcutt

"I tried to create poses that felt like Boga was a very fast animal, with lots of flowing S-curves."
—GLEN MCINTOSH

◀▲ UTC: UTAPAU 10TH LEVEL CONTROL CENTER SEQUENCE, LIZARD STUDIES
McIntosh

"I added some cloud shadows creeping across the dunes to give it a sense of life and motion."—BRETT NORTHCUTT

BOGA ANIMATION

JULY 2004

Rallied by Coleman, lead animators Jamy Wheless, Virginie d'Annoville, Tim Harrington, Paul Kavanaugh, Virgil Manning, Scott Benza, and Glen McIntosh strive to create fluid performances for CG vehicles, droids, aliens, humanoids, and creatures. Having come into conceptual existence more than two years ago, the lizard now known as Boga is one of the major challenges for this department—and for McIntosh in particular. "Before diving into the CG animation, I created some rough sketches," McIntosh explains, "a colored render, and a brief character profile to help define the Boga's attitude and mannerisms. I think if he stretched his neck and tail out, he'd be almost fifty feet long! The tricky part has been making him fast enough to catch Grievous's speeder, while maintaining the weight and physics of a creature with that much mass!"

THE GALAXIES OPERA HOUSE, ACT III

JUNE–JULY, 2004

As the date of additional photography pickups approaches—August 23 to September 3 at Shepperton Studios in England—alien garbs and costumes are finalized. Indeed, the new opera-staircase shot includes Lucas's first cameo in the *Star Wars* saga. As Baron N. Papanoida, he'll be seen next to his daughter Katie (Chi Eekway).

▲ FEMALE ISHI 02
Jun

▲ BARON COSTUME 01
Jun

▲ RYSTALL COSTUME 02 & 3
Jun

▲ TOONBUCK COSTUME 01
Jun

◄ BARON N. PAPANOIDA COSTUME CONCEPT
Jun

▲ BARON N. PAPANOIDA FINAL COSTUME
Jun

206

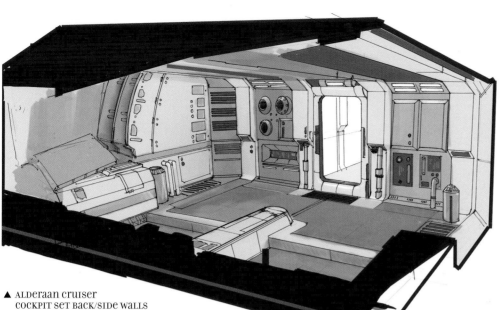

▲ alderaan cruiser
cockpit set back/side walls
Jaeger

▼ cruiser landed on alderaan
Church

July 2004

One of Lucas's additional scenes requires a new locale: the cockpit of the Alderaan space cruiser. As the ship heads back to Coruscant, Obi-Wan, Yoda, and Bail Organa receive a message there summoning the latter to a special Senate session. "Nobody had ever seen the Rebel blockade runner cockpit," Jaeger says, "but George had already created its parameters, which matched those of the Episode I Jedi cruiser, before we started the design. Because this room wasn't as wide as the front of the actual Alderaan ship, we reasoned that this is the center cockpit of perhaps three rooms. So we only see three windows, but there would be two more on each side."

▲ alderaan cruiser
entry door detail
Jaeger

"George wanted a really simple costume with little decoration. So I created a simple shape for a desert costume, with a short cape and Middle East type of hat."
—Jun

▶ bail cruiser cockpit revisions
Jaeger

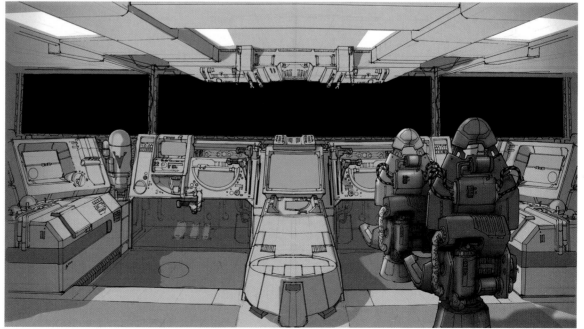

▲ MUSTAFAR PLANET CONCEPT 02
Church

"This was an extremely late addition, created when George said 'I want Mustafar orbiting a gas planet.'"—CHURCH

◄ CROP OF THE ANIMATED DIGITAL MUSTAFAR CYCLORAMA
Northcutt

"Roger Guyett [visual effects supervisor] suggested that we do a trench, because for the teaser trailer he wanted to use some of ILM's practical models."
—TIEMENS

▼ MUSTAFAR FLEA TRENCH, REVISED
Tiemens

On April 13 and 28, two key meetings take place in the Skywalker Ranch art department. Their purpose is to forever pin down the geography of Mustafar. To create what they hope are the most cohesive and fantastic landscapes possible—and ones that tie together all the concept art and principal photography—Tiemens, McBride, and Dusseault create a series of paintings on top of Euisung Lee's animatics derived from earlier concept paintings. "This was in part done by combining dramatic elements," Dusseault explains, "such as exploding oceans of lava, razor-sharp rock formations, and by basically reinventing hell's inferno. For the cyclorama, Erik, Aaron, and I rebuilt the entire sequence—every shot—all the exteriors. Working with rough 3-D models, we tried to find every angle that would match the photographic plate—and then bridge all that together." To their relief, Lucas approves their work at the second meeting, and over the next several months Mustafar makes the jump from concept to photo-real.

▲ MUSTAFAR, NEW LAYOUT
Tiemens

▼ MLP.140: MUSTAFAR LANDING PLATFORM
Tiemens

▲ MCB.180: MUSTAFAR CONTROL CENTER BALCONY SHOTS (PAINTING OVER ANIMATICS)
McBride

◀ LOW BUILDING, MODEL SHOP REFERENCE
Church

"Once I knew that ILM was going to make practical models instead of digital, I had to really sit down like an architect and design how the buildings sit." —CHURCH

▶ UTAPAU SINKHOLE SECTION
ILM model shop

UTAPAU CITY SYSTEM

JUNE–SEPTEMBER 2004

In the animatics department, Lucas sometimes re-examines old concept paintings and extracts parts of them for the scenes he's working on. Church or Tiemens then takes these excerpts and cleans them up, so the animartist can work on a clean plate. A similar process of clarification is used in creating reference for ILM's practical model shop. Under the supervision of Brian Gernand and chief model maker Michael Lynch, the model crew of the Utapau 1/90 scale model included: Mark Buck, Fon Davis, Nelson Hall, Danny Wagner, Grant Imahara, Pierre Mauer, and Randy Ottenberg.

▼▶ UTAPAU 1/90 SCALE SINKHOLE SECTION
ILM model shop

"AT LAST WE WILL HAVE REVENGE"

DECEMBER 2003–OCTOBER 2004

"The idea behind the archaeological frieze in Palpatine's office," Tiemens says, "is that it depicts an event. George was very clear about making it a dynamic and somewhat gory scene of Jedi and aliens and warriors fighting each other. Richard [Miller] created the sculpture of this. He's very thoughtful and careful, and I worked with him to achieve a modello look—the kind of things that students might do in terra-cotta before doing their final sculpture. Then we aged it and gave it cracks."

▲ BAS-RELIEF SCULPTURE, DETAILS
Miller

▲ BAS-RELIEF IN PALPATINE'S ANTECHAMBER
Tiemens

"The Star Wars *saga is like a symphony, which has recurring themes."*—LUCAS

▲ BAS-RELIEF SCULPTURE
Miller

▼ MACE WINDU, PALPATINE'S OFFICE ENTRANCE
Church

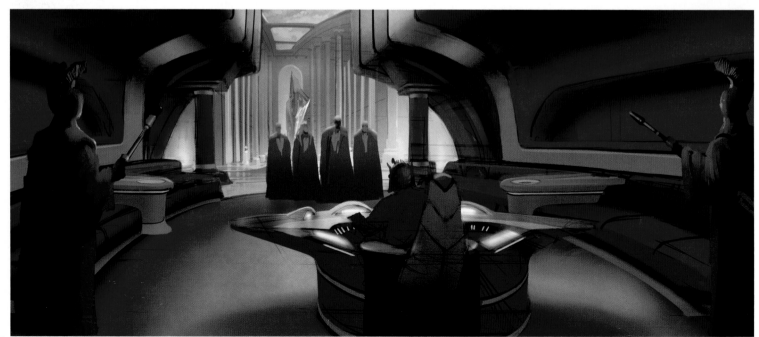

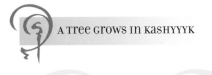
A TREE GROWS IN KASHYYYK

▲▼ KASHYYYK TREE PRACTICAL MODEL, DETAILS
ILM model shop

DECEMBER 2003–OCTOBER 2004

Among the last CG sequences to be tackled are those of Kashyyyk. Indeed, it is only in May 2004 that Rob Coleman returns to Fox Studios Australia to record the necessary footage of the Wookiee extras, while Lucas tapes Peter Mayhew (Chewbacca) in July. Because the sequences on that planet are running long, the scene in which Yoda creates a diversion by feigning madness, enabling Wookiees to attack clone troopers, is cut. The Kashyyyk tree practical model was built under the supervision of Brian Gernand and chief model maker Don Bies with a crew that included John Berg, Tom Vukmanic, and Gritsada Satjawatcharaphong.

▲ KASHYYYK CITY, DETAIL 03
Church

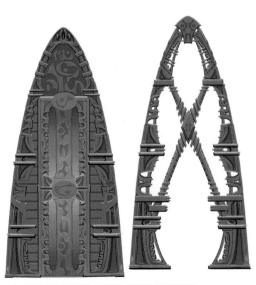

▲ KASHYYYK TREE, LARGE-SCALE ARCHWAY FOR MODEL SHOP REFERENCE
McBride

217

▲▶ coruscant padmé veranda at night
Maeda/Dusseault

"This is a night-version cyclorama. I used over 500 buildings to make a 360-degree environment."
—TOSHIYUKI MAEDA

▼ scene 55, anakin & padmé
post-dream cyclorama
Dusseault

▼ CJG: gunship cyclorama, digi-matte painting
Thorngren

▶ CJG: coruscant jedi gunship cyclorama, concept painting
Tiemens

"For the scene where Yoda and Mace are in the gunship, George said he wanted golden shafts piercing the buildings. Then he wanted them to turn the corner and head toward stormier skies."—TIEMENS

DIGI-MATTE CORUSCANT

By mid-2004 the digi-matte painting department consists of thirty or so people—about three times what it would be normally for even a large visual effects film. "Rick and George weren't shy about spreading the word—they really wanted a deep bench," says department supervisor Jonathan Harb, who has brought in artists from as far away as Japan, Sweden, England, New Zealand, Canada, and China. "I recruit people who are low maintenance and who have very broad skill sets," he adds, noting that "just the omitted shots of this film equal the quantity of shots usually necessary for a good-sized visual effects show." Indeed, as six months remain on *Star Wars*: Episode III *Revenge of the Sith*, many vistas remain to be completed. This book must now come to an end, but the finished movie will contain the last of the artworks—the culmination of the thousands created in the three-year imaginings of an inspired crew—as envisioned by Lucas.

▲ FBC. 680: FEDCRUISER BRIDGE CRASH
Thorngren

▼ CRASH LANDING ON CORUSCANT
Church

▼ reнab center exterior,
 FINAL CONCEPT (INSET)
 Church

"The rehab center is the tallest building on Coruscant and sits over an ocean of needlelike buildings" —NORTHCUTT

"We're going to push the limits of matte painting!" —LUCAS

▲ STORMY CYCLORAMA FROM ATOP THE JEDI TEMPLE
Maeda/Dusseault

▼ REHAB CENTER (SITH TOWER) DIGI-MATTE PAINTING
Northcutt

"The most important thing for me, personally, when the film is released, is that it's a breakthrough in terms of being visually breathtaking and emotionally powerful." —MCCALLUM

ACKNOWLEDGMENTS

SPECIAL THANKS TO: RICK MCCALLUM, FOR HIS ADVICE, HUMOR, and for giving me the OK stamp to write this book. And to David Craig, for inspiring all the artists, taking them down the road they hadn't traveled; Robert E. Barnes, whose grotesque sculpture truly tricked me; Ryan Church, for his insights into his art and the process; Fay David—very simply, this book could not have been finished without her help; Iain McCaig, who arrived on the scene like a tornado; John Goodson, for the great stories about the special effects of yesteryear; Erik Tiemens, who links up this story with the rest of art history; and T. J. Frame, Warren Fu, Alex Jaeger, Sang Jun Lee, Aaron McBride, Michael Murnane, Derek Thompson, Danny Wagner, and Feng Zhu, who patiently spoke about each of their artworks.

In Australia, thanks to: Trisha Biggar, for explanations of her craft; Colette Birrell, for help with all things art department; Gavin Bocquet, who united hundreds of artworks and gave me a master's class on production; Dave Elsey and Rebecca Hunt, for their responses to follow-up e-mails; and Peter Russell, who instructed me in the finer details of set construction.

At Industrial Light & Magic: Rob Coleman, who early on kept reminding me this was an animated movie; Jonathan Harb, Yanick Dusseault, Toshiyuki Maeda, Brett Northcutt, and Johan Thorngren, who gave their time and notes to the book; and everyone in the animation department, whose biweekly meetings with George were invaluable; and to Christy Castellano for tracking down those elusive assets.

At Lucasfilm, thanks to: Amy Gary, for charging to the fore; Tina Mills, who gathered together every image with humor and precision, and Scott Carter for photographing key artwork; Iain R. Morris, for his magnificent art direction and helping out a little with the design!; Howard Roffman, for as always providing learned council; and Sue Rostoni, for being my companion-in-arms. At Del Rey: Steve Saffel, for having confidence; Keith Clayton, Erich Schoeneweiss, Dave Stevenson, and Sylvain Michaelis, for taking the words and the images and bringing them together.

And special thanks to George Lucas, who allowed me to observe his three-year interactions with, and directions to, the artists, designers, and animators—and who agreed to write the foreword even while in the home stretch of finishing his movie.

▲ TATOOINE DIGI-MATTE PAINTING
Benoit Pelchat

NOTES & INDEX

Part I: Quotes are from personal interviews conducted with Robert Barnes, Ryan Church, Fay David, T. J. Frame, Warren Fu, John Goodson, Alex Jaeger, Iain McCaig, Michael Patrick Murnane, Sang Jun Lee, Erik Tiemens, Derek Thompson, Danny Wagner, and Feng Zhu in the Skywalker Ranch art department from March to October 2003. Other sources include personal notes written during art department meetings from July 2002 to June 2003, and art department supervisor Fay David's notes from April 2002 to June 2003.

Part II: Quotes are from personal interviews with Trisha Biggar, Gavin Bocquet, Matt Connors, Dave Elsey, Clive Memmott, and Peter Russell conducted during principal photography at Fox Studios, Australia, from July to September 2003. Additional quotes from Trisha Biggar, Greg Hajdu, and others come from electronic press-kit interviews conducted by documentary director Tippy Bushkin at the same place during the same time period. Additional quotes from Dave Elsey are from emails dated June 2004.

Part III: Quotes are from personal interviews with Ryan Church, Rob Coleman, Fay David, Yanick Dusseault, Jonathan Harb, Alex Jaeger, Toshiyuki Maeda, Aaron McBride, Glen McIntosh, Brett Northcutt, Erik Tiemens, Johan Thorngren, and Jamy Wheless conducted at Industrial Light & Magic, in August 2004. Additional Rob Coleman quotes are from an interview conducted by Tippy Bushkin in August 2003 at Fox Studios, Australia.

Quotes from George Lucas are from personal interviews conducted in March 2003 and June 2004, and notes taken during art department meetings, on the set, and at ILM from July 2002 to October 2004. Rick McCallum quotes are from many personal interviews conducted from April 2002 to October 2004.

Selected List of Concept Artists' Materials

Drawing: no. 2 pencil, mechanical pencil 0.3 or 0.5, HB or 2b lead; Bic black ball point pen, Gelly Roll brown and black pen, Pilot HI-TEC-C 0.3 or 0.5 pen, black fountain pen; Pantone Tria marker inks with cotton wipes, Prisma-color markers (many artists used a selection of cool grays), Carré hard pastels

Paper: Letraset marker paper, Bienfang graphics 360 marker paper, Arches water color paper, just plain ol' 8.5 by 11 inches copy-paper, various toned papers (Stonehenge gray and buff)

Highlights/paints: white gel pen, white-out pen, gouache, acrylic, Windsor & Newton sable and University white synthetic brushes (rounds and flats, various sizes)

Key frames and storyboards: Col-Erase blue and pencils, cheap plastic mechanical pencil, ball point pen, black Sharpies, Prisma-color gray markers

Software: Painter 7, 8 & 9, Photoshop 7 (mostly over scanned drawings)

▼ CLONE TROOPER CONCEPT
Zhu